THE CONCLUSION OF THE *FLOWERS IN DECEMBER* TRILOGY

SECOND chance

Books by Jane Suen

Children of the Future
Murder Creek

FLOWERS IN DECEMBER TRILOGY
Flowers in December
Coming Home
Second Chance

ALTERATIONS TRILOGY
Alterations
Game Changer
Primal Will

SHORT STORIES
Beginnings and Endings: A Selection of Short Stories

THE CONCLUSION OF THE *FLOWERS IN DECEMBER* TRILOGY

SECOND chance

JANE SUEN

SECOND CHANCE: The Conclusion of the *Flowers in December* Trilogy

Jane Suen books are available for order through Ingram Press Catalogues.

www.janesuen.com

Printed in the United States of America

First Printing: December 2019

Library of Congress Control Number: 2019919459

Paperback ISBN: 978-1-951002-05-3
Audiobook ISBN: 978-1-951002-06-0
Ebook ISBN: 978-1-951002-04-6

To the readers who have enjoyed my books

and

To my baby sister.

This one's for you!

Chapter 1

SHE FELT SOFT hairs brush against her leg a moment before Isabella leaped on the couch and joined her.

"Well, Happy New Year to you, too," said Mary Ann, her lips brushing the silky white hairs as she planted a kiss on the cat's head. Mary Ann had settled in for a few minutes of quiet time to write, curled up on the couch, a steaming mug of hot chocolate within easy reach on the table. Putting her pen and notebook aside, Mary Ann gave Isabella some love—rather some extra love—on this special day, as the cat nestled and carved out a snug spot next to her. She petted her cat, feeling the warmth of Isabella's small body and hearing the soft, contented purr.

Mary Ann glanced at the resolutions she had scribbled on the pad. It helped to see it in writing. Made it more real, accountable. She always started with her best intentions, but knew most of them would fall to the wayside long before the year was over. She'd learned a long time ago not to be too hard on herself and to celebrate when she achieved just one thing, even if it was the smallest of goals.

On the notepad, Mary Ann had written one word: love.

Her grandfather had shown her the meaning of love after her father died. Thinking of him brought a familiar ache to her heart. Grandpa Evert had passed almost two years ago. He had been the one person she loved more than anyone, since her father died when she was six and her mother remarried to Steve a few years later. Her stepfather—the thought of him, and that word, stepfather, repulsed her. He had forced Mary Ann to say it, call him *Dad*, and then he'd watch as she choked on it, spitting it out. Her mother never understood why Mary Ann was so stubborn. Why her daughter wouldn't accept *Dad*.

But Grandpa did—he understood and knew Mary Ann better than anyone. He practically raised her. Mary Ann had spent as much time with him as she could. He and Grandma lived in the same neighborhood and within easy walking distance, and Mary Ann would pass by their house on the way to the elementary school. She treasured the memories of those happy days.

After school, Mary Ann would race to their front door, her skinny legs flying. She was always hungry right about this time, and they took care of her. Grandma made sure she had a snack, the homemade kind—not something you'd buy in a plastic wrapper to tear open. More often than not, it'd be a chewy cookie and a glass of milk. Grandma used to say, "Let's not spoil your appetite." When Mary Ann finished and wiped the crumbs off her face, Grandpa would be waiting in his favorite easy chair. They'd sit and chat for a while; he always wanted to know how her day went.

Sometimes Grandma would join them or sit in her chair and knit. Sometimes Mary Ann stayed with them for an entire weekend visit.

Mary Ann didn't mind homework, though they didn't call it "work" for nothing. Grandpa made sure she stayed on top of things and didn't slack off. His motto was "homework first," so he'd make sure she did it. If she had questions, he was more than happy to help. Grandpa didn't lavish praises on Mary Ann when she did well in school. But he'd ask for her report card, taking his time to put on his glasses and look over her grades. The most he ever said was "good." Once Mary Ann overheard Grandpa talk about her, saying she was "smart as a whip," and she felt happy and all warm and wonderful inside.

She smiled, remembering Grandpa. He was a tough old man—both outside and in: wiry and without an ounce of extra fat on his lean frame, and possessing a resilience born of survival through hard times. His parents struggled during the Great Depression—difficult times that almost tore apart the fabric of their family. They were proud folks and refused to take government handouts and avoided the shame of going on welfare. They didn't buy new clothes for a long time. Instead, his mother patched their worn-out clothing.

The family lived mainly on soup and bread. His mother struck up an acquaintance with the butcher and bartered with him, taking in his laundry and doing some sewing in exchange for soup bones and occasional scraps of meat. Nothing was wasted. Old vegetables were never tossed away unless they were rotten. Odds and ends of veggies found their way into the soup. It'd simmer for hours on the stove; the delicious smell wafting in the air as his mother lifted the cover, adding scraps and stirring the mixture, mixing in seasonings and herbs to flavor the broth.

Mary Ann loved to hear Grandpa's stories of the hardships they endured during those Great Depression years, and how they survived and grew closer through the experience. They lived through it, became stronger. She teared up, glancing at his picture, the frame propped on the table against the living room wall. Even in his nineties, Grandpa looked handsome. A head full of shocking white hair, a deeply lined face, and just a trace of a smile below stern, proud eyes.

Chapter 2

THE STARK WINTRY scene was a reminder to dress warmly. Mary Ann pulled on a thermal shirt and tucked it into her jeans. The weather reporter warned of another storm brewing, with a snowfall of likely a foot or more. Walking out her door, she scrunched her face to gaze up at the sky. Dense gray clouds had blocked out the sun. She shivered, zipping up her jacket.

The holidays had almost depleted her food supplies. Mary Ann needed to stock up and refill the pantry. She'd meant to go earlier, but the week had passed. A hankering for a bowl of hot soup and slow-cooked ingredients simmered for hours came to mind. She swallowed in anticipation. She wasn't up to cooking today.

Mary Ann was ready for the winter to be over. The last few weeks had been bitter cold—the kind that cuts through, chilling to the bones. Yet she hadn't minded it too much as long as the sun was out. Now, Mary Ann dreaded the approaching storm and the upheaval it would bring. It was best to reach the market before another stampede cleared the shelves. She should be getting used to the weather by now, living in this small mountain town.

When Mary Ann opened the flower shop in Rocky Flats, she became a member of its business community and the town itself. Connor's mom and the other folks she met had welcomed her warmly. Mary Ann got to know them when they ordered flowers for birthdays, graduations, jobs, marriages, holidays—occasions for celebrations, as well as for get-wells and the passing of life.

This time of year especially—home, family, the meaning of life, and Christmas brought back fond memories for Mary Ann: of her childhood with her father, those years she had with Grandpa Evert and Grandma, the happy days of long ago. Memories tugged at Mary Ann's heart and transported her to a time and place that was magical, so many years ago—to the life she'd had as a child, the joys she'd experienced. This quaint and charming town had brought back those special childhood memories.

Mary Ann stopped by the grocery store for essential staples: coffee, eggs, milk, cheese, bread, and to be sure—something for Isabella. Quickly maneuvering down the familiar aisles, Mary Ann got her shopping done before the rush.

The fresh market was her next stop. Mary Ann occasionally shopped at this place for healthy prepared food and organic produce. Today, she fixated on soup. Pushing her cart to the counter, she eyed the selections: navy bean and vegetarian chili. There was nothing like a nutritious, hearty bowl of soup, and theirs was blue-ribbon quality. A little pricey, but totally worth it. Mary Ann bent down to read the list of ingredients.

"Mary Ann," a masculine voice called out.

She almost jumped. Immersed in her thoughts, she hadn't expected to run into anyone. The voice sounded familiar.

He dashed toward her, crossing the gap in quick strides.

Straightening up, she hid her fluster. "Connor—" she said, blinking and trying not to stare.

"Yours truly," said Connor. He grinned, his hands touching his chest, as though to hide his racing heartbeat. The market logo was displayed across the front of his green apron with monogrammed leaves.

Mary Ann blushed. "You ... haven't ... left town?" she stuttered, apparently suddenly interested in the apron.

"Still here."

"What about your job in the city ... your home there?" It took a moment for Mary Ann to digest this. Connor was still here. She had tried to push him out of sight and out of mind. Yet here he was, beaming at her, in flesh and blood—and looking *too* darn good, as her primal brain kicked in, taking instant notice.

"I quit my job and moved back here."

"But why?" She kept her tone neutral, as she glanced at his face, searching for clues.

"I decided to put the big city life behind me—for good."

Hearing this news, Mary Ann's stomach fluttered. He'd left the city for good? She felt as if she stood at a crossroad, wavering between going straight or turning left or right. Her logical brain took over her thinking. *Remember what happened when you let your guard down? Opened your heart?* Emotions swirled, stirring up the anger, the hurt, and the disappointment. "So … you came back to stay—"

"I'm at my parents' home," said Connor. "With Tom," he added.

The mention of Connor's orange tabby cat brought a slight curl to her lips, and then a bit of a frown as Mary Ann recalled his worries about Tom. Connor had come back from the city, and they had last talked on Christmas Eve about taking Tom to the vet.

"Did you take Tom to see Doc Carlson?" she asked, concern in her voice.

"Doc gave us the first available appointment and saw Tom right away. He puts his animal patients first, even during the holidays," said Connor, taking a deep breath. "He's a skilled diagnostician, sharper than the other vets I took Tom to. You're lucky to have Doc Carlson in this small town. He has his fingers on the pulse and knew what was wrong."

"Is Tom better now?" She didn't have to ask, judging from the cheery grin Connor threw her. This unexpected run-in took her by surprise. Just like the last time she saw him on Christmas Eve, when Connor popped into her flower shop after not hearing from him for four months when he went back to the city after his mother's funeral in town. She pursed her lips, a wisp of anger creeping back.

"Doc told me animals *can* grieve. Tom was my mother's constant companion. Mom loved her orange-striped tomboy dearly." After a moment of silence, Connor brushed a piece of fuzz off the apron, adjusting the strap. "Doc said the cat would have sensed *my* grief, too."

Mary Ann shook her head. This was not the place to give him a piece of her mind. The holidays had calmed her, took some sting out of her seething anger. Besides, Connor had apologized and seemed genuinely sorry. But was she ready to forgive him?

Chapter 3

"MARY ANN—" HIS voice was soft. Seeing her again took Connor back to that day when they had met at the flower shop. The petite brunette who had greeted him was professional and poised, yet compassionate. Mary Ann had made the floral arrangements for his mother's funeral, selecting the white flowers which were his mother's favorite color. That beautiful girl with the radiant smile had warmed Connor's heart in the dark days that followed, and she'd been his strength when he was weak with grief.

"You enjoy working here?" she finally asked.

"It's good. I'm usually in the back, in the kitchen. Not full-time, just a few hours when they need me."

"You're right at home in the kitchen," said Mary Ann. She recalled the time he had invited her, Mrs. Rainer—his mother's dear friend and neighbor—and the pastor and his daughter Eva over for dinner. It was his way of thanking them for being a part of his mother's life, and afterward, the beautiful funeral service. He had even invited Isabella to meet Tom. Mary Ann had never known a man who was so comfortable in the kitchen. Connor had explained he owed it to his mother, who taught him how to cook when he was so small he had to stand on a stepstool to watch her.

"I'm the soup cook, preparing vegetables from what we have in the market, picking those that are older and using them up first." He ventured a smile. "They make tasty broths, and I make them just like my mother did."

She stepped up to the counter and scrutinized the day's soup offerings. "Which one do you recommend?" Mary Ann held a sturdy paper to-go container in her hand.

He leaned in, squinting at the labels. Connor had put them on himself. It was an excuse to move closer to Mary Ann. "What are you in the mood for?"

"Something hearty and fulfilling."

He resisted the urge to tell her he could hold her, warm her up, right here and now, in the middle of the store. "Do you like red or white?"

Mary Ann laughed. "We're talking about soups, not wine, right?"

Connor loved to see her like that. The way Mary Ann's beautiful brown eyes lit up, the tiny crinkles at the edges. The way her perfect lips parted, the cute dimples appearing on her cheeks. He'd never tire of looking at her—her face, her smiles, her laughter.

He picked up the ladle and stirred the bean soup, hoping she wouldn't notice the shaking in his hand.

She studied the bean soup before she answered, watching the contents swirl, dispersing the navy beans that had settled to the bottom. "Tonight, I have a hankering for a rich, red soup."

Connor pointed to the vegetarian chili. "This fits the bill. It's tasty and thick, in a tomato base packed with red beans, onions, celery, bell peppers, and meatless crumbles."

"Not too spicy or hot?"

"Green chilies hot enough?" teased Connor.

Mary Ann's eyes widened.

"Just kidding."

Mary Ann glanced at the chili, then smiled. "Okay, I'll try this."

"You'll like the chili," said Connor with a wink, reaching for the container in her hand. He filled it and popped on a lid. As he handed her the soup, his fingers brushed hers lightly. Their eyes met and locked in a gaze. Her touch. Her eyes. Her blush. He was smitten all over again.

She felt a zing. A definite redness colored her cheeks.

She nodded, noticing how Connor looked different now. Gone was the designer suit and expensive tie; instead, he wore a soft cotton shirt and jeans. But it wasn't just his attire that had changed. There was something else about Connor. She couldn't quite spell it out, but he sported a relaxed posture, appearing content and more at ease. Even his gaze was softer … and a sparkle was in his eyes.

"How'd you end up here?" said Mary Ann.

Connor chuckled. "I like shopping here for fresh organic fruits and vegetables. I bumped into the owner one day, and well … she remembered me." He paused. "I didn't know she was the owner here when she and I first met at your flower shop, the day I went to see you on Christmas Eve. It was crowded, and people were pushing and shoving. She was the old woman that I escorted to the front counter." He grunted, shaking his head. "You should have seen how she beamed when she saw me again, here in this market. She mentioned that business had picked up. They didn't advertise for a position, and they didn't really have one with enough hours to qualify for full-time, but they needed someone part-time in the kitchen."

"And that suited you—"

"That's right." Connor nodded. "I love to cook, and this interested me. Besides, I don't need the money from working full-time. Where else can I get paid to do what I enjoy?"

This brought a curve to Mary Ann's lips. This Connor was different. The other Connor, well … he wasn't in a good frame of mind. He'd even admitted that much.

"Welcome back," said Mary Ann, blurting out the words as a gesture of goodwill, despite the trace of bitterness that lingered. When he'd invited her to supper on Christmas Day, she didn't accept, and she didn't respond right away until it was too late. Her pride, her ego, whatever it was, had held her back. Connor had apologized, but it hadn't been enough. Was she bent on exacting revenge, making him suffer for the pain he caused? She had another option on Christmas Day: an earlier invitation from Ron, the owner of the hardware store. She couldn't very well cancel on Ron at the last moment—on Christmas of all days. She had guessed that Ron was interested in her that time at his store, when he shared his dreams of expansion, and so his invite wasn't unexpected.

Mary Ann had first met Connor on the day he arrived in town and talked to her about the flower arrangements for his mother's funeral. He was in town for three more weeks to take care of things. During that period, he had invited Mary Ann over for dinner, and they'd spent more time together, dining at Manini's restaurant before his departure. But Connor had left abruptly and without saying goodbye. When he came back to town again a few days ago, his apology on Christmas Eve was small consolation for the bitter disappointment she had experienced. Mary Ann had sworn not to fall into that trap again.

Connor looked like he was working up the nerve to say something. Perhaps another apology? Whatever it was, Mary Ann suddenly decided she wasn't interested in hearing it. Not now.

"I need to run and do all my shopping before the storm hits," said Mary Ann, her voice terse as she set the soup container on the counter, freeing her hands to reposition the contents of her overflowing reusable grocery bag, moving celery stalks and a bag of oranges about to spill over the brim. She hastily turned toward the checkout lane. "I still have to stop by the flower shop to put up a sign and close early."

"Norma minding the store?"

"Yes." Mary Ann adjusted the straps of her full bag, redistributing the weight digging into her shoulder.

"Old man winter is still kicking. I'm afraid it'll be another bad one."

"Well, the florist business has slowed down after the holidays. I'll keep the shop closed for a few days, with this storm brewing." Mary Ann moved away, joining the growing line in front of the register. "I need to get going."

He nodded, watching her as she reached the cashier, paid, and walked out of the market, carrying her shopping bag. The curls in her long hair bounced with each step, soft and free-flowing. He remembered the way she'd looked the first time he saw her in the flower shop. She had tied her curls back in a ponytail. He liked seeing her hair down. There was a lump in his throat as he stared at Mary Ann's retreating figure.

Even as she moved out of earshot, Connor still blurted out, "Come back again." The words fell on empty air, lost as she opened the door.

Chapter 4

CONNOR HAD AN urge to run after Mary Ann as she walked out of the market, before her trim, petite frame disappeared from view. He'd missed his chance to tell her how he felt. He missed her already. He longed to gaze into her lovely eyes framed by soft long lashes, to hear her voice, to be with her. He wanted to draw her closer to him. So close that she'd feel the thump of his beating heart.

Seeing Mary Ann brought her back into his mind, squarely in front. He had tried not to think of her these last few days, to leave things as they were, to come to terms with the fact she hadn't accepted his invite to spend Christmas with him. Had he lost her?

In his heart of hearts, she had never left. He had held on to the connection in his mind, as he suffered and grieved his loss, struggling through those days, weeks, and months after his mother died. But he'd never told Mary Ann how he felt. How could he then? He could barely hold on to himself.

Connor had experienced the darkest period of his life in those four months when he went back to the city. He lost his zest for life. His ambition to climb the corporate ladder no longer fueled his drive. With no one to share his success, he felt an emptiness, a void. He had pulled back into himself, withdrawn away from Tom, who he'd inherited from his mom. A part of him deep down knew he had nothing to give Mary Ann. If he had reached out, he'd be leaning on her, a burden to her. Many a time he'd thought of calling her, but he'd resisted. Instead, he replayed the times they had spent together, keeping Mary Ann alive in his mind and, in this way, she stayed with Connor during his darkest moments.

He fell into a bleak existence, absent of the comfort of good food, not even making simple quick meals. He forgot to feed Tom on more than one occasion, leaving his bowl empty. When he did, it was the cheap cat food from the grocery store. Connor himself skipped meals. It became a task, a mundane shuffling of cardboard-tasting food from vending machines, frozen dinners, and the occasional late-night drive-thru to squelch his hunger with greasy fried food. In between, he stockpiled snacks from the stores that sold items for a dollar, amazed to find selections that changed from week to week.

Sometime in late November, he made a stop at the pet store to buy more nutritious cat food. The night before, Connor had flinched, jerking his hand away, when his fingers felt the cat's thin, bony body under the fur. The realization had sunk in—Tom had lost weight—and with it, Connor's shame and dread. A heavy ache stuck in his throat.

He had sunk to the floor and held Tom in his arms, sobbing as he rocked back and forth.

He knew then it would take more than food to bring Tom back to his old self—and himself, too.

On Christmas Day, up until the last moment after the other guests had arrived for supper, he'd still held hopes she'd walk in the door. He almost went to see Mary Ann at the flower shop afterward. But he nixed the idea, turning around before he set foot in her store. What right did he have to expect she'd come running to him? The distance that had separated them for the four months was of his making. He had pushed her away and hurt her. He should have … well, it was too late to be rethinking this. What was done was done.

Connor had dreaded this holiday, his first Christmas alone, with only Tom by his side. He had run into Alana, his neighbor Dottie Rainer's long-estranged daughter. He had invited them, along with the pastor and his daughter, for Christmas supper. It had been a sad, but bittersweet Christmas, one without his mother. But she would have approved of her only child and friends gathered together to honor her. Coming home had been the right decision.

He had kept busy, which helped to push away the melancholy and dispel the self-pity.

People made resolutions for the New Year, full of promises and good intentions. Connor had made his— leaving the city, his job, and his condo—coming back to his small hometown to start anew. It was bold, a major decision. A turning point.

Connor hadn't expected to run into Mary Ann today. She looked good, but seemed a bit frazzled. He had wondered how she was doing. Their chance meeting, the brief conversation fanned the tiny flame in his heart—injected it with a breath of fresh oxygen. This time, he wanted to make another effort, try again. He would go slow, to do whatever it took.

He had climbed the corporate ladder. He had fixed his eyes on the goal, and the office with the window was a special perk along the way. After his mother died, it had all changed. He searched his inner self and knew his heart wasn't in it. What if he rose higher and made it to the expansive executive corner office? They'd only want more of him, more than the sixty-plus hours a week he'd already given. What other price did he have to pay to gain entry to the top level?

Connor had left and never looked back. Now he'd settled into the slower pace of life with Tom; a life he'd lost so long ago, one that didn't suck the life out of him.

Mary Ann. He remembered the times they spent together. They were like precious gems. They were scenes he'd played and replayed to remind him of the good times. Connor couldn't help grinning, feeling the quickening of his heart as his face lit up, his hopes raised. Mary Ann—he wanted to cry out her name, dance with her, take her in his arms. Oh, *stop* … she wasn't his.

The things that held him back raised their heads. The doubts. A voice of caution. Remember the disappointment?

A chill chased the butterflies in Connor's stomach at the

thought. Was there someone else in her life now? He had so much he wanted to say to Mary Ann. Things he wanted to ask her in person. But Connor hadn't brought it up today, hadn't wanted to break the cheerful mood. He didn't want to risk her answer or her rejection.

Chapter 5

NORMA LOOKED OUT the window. The heavy clouds heralded the oncoming storm. She had to stay at work, but called her husband, Stan, to pick up food and supplies. Occasionally the weatherman was wrong, but something told Norma he was right about this one. The last customer had just left when she heard a ping on her cell phone, Mary Ann texting she was on her way.

In a few minutes, the door opened and Mary Ann breezed through. She was rushing, panting. "We can close early," said Mary Ann, tossing her head toward the darkened sky and threatening clouds outside.

Norma nodded. "I called Stan. It looks like a bad one's coming."

"I'll put up a sign while you close up," hollered Mary Ann, disappearing into the back room.

Norma brought the chalkboard easel display on the sidewalk inside the shop and closed out the cash register.

"How's this?" said Mary Ann as she came back, holding up the hastily written sign, "Closed due to inclement weather."

"It works," said Norma.

Mary Ann scurried to prop it on the storefront window, then flipped the sign on the front door.

"How long will we be closed?" said Norma.

"Tomorrow is Friday, and we have the weekend coming up. Let's see how the storm goes. I'd like to open by Monday."

Norma nodded. "Are you all set for the storm?"

"I've got enough food to last me and Isabella for a few days."

"We're used to this." said Norma with a reassuring nod. "You'll figure it out and learn how things are around here."

"I'm really liking it here."

"You wouldn't be talking about a certain young man, would you?" teased Norma.

"Now, why would you say that?" said Mary Ann with a throaty giggle. She still hadn't told Norma what happened with her and Ron on New Year's Eve. And she didn't mention seeing Connor a few minutes ago.

Chapter 6

MARY ANN HAD wondered what it would be like to kiss Ron at the stroke of midnight on New Year's Eve. She had built up the moment after their "date" at his cabin on Christmas Day. In her heart of hearts, Mary Ann was a romantic. Although, she hid it behind her no-nonsense business exterior.

She had imagined it would be like this: like the soft petals of a flower glistening with dew, her lips parted. She felt his warm breath as their lips met in this first kiss. The touch was magical, sending little waves of pleasure through her body. Her eyes remained closed. Mary Ann opened into the kiss and the embrace as the man wrapped his arms around her. She reached up to clasp the back of his neck, pulling him closer while her fingers intertwined in his thick hair, tugging it playfully, but not yanking it.

She lost track of the time as she kissed and didn't care. Keeping her eyes closed, she explored the new senses: the lingering smell of his cologne, the scratchy tickle of his stubble on her smooth skin, the warmth of his arms around her, the taste of his lips. Mary Ann murmured involuntarily, lost in the moment.

When they broke away, Mary Ann would notice the shy gaze of adoration on his face. The heart-thumping, utter devotion of a man in love. It was sweetness, joy, all wrapped up. His eyes were fixed on her. As he gazed, the grin never left his face.

His warm eyes spoke to her without a single word. She returned it with a slight curve of her lips and another tender kiss.

STOP. Rewind.

But it *didn't* happen like this. *Not with Ron.*

Mary Ann was not the touchy-feely type of person to begin with. After her father died, her mother was quick to marry the first man who showed an interest in her and who held a steady-paying job. She wasn't cut out for the "single mother struggling with child" role. Her mother was shrewd and calculating, and she knew her value as a woman, a commodity with her clock ticking. Men looking for younger women to date or women who didn't have a child, didn't look her way once they found out she came as a package of two.

Her mother knew the older she got, the slimmer the pickings. So, when her stepfather-to-be came along, a middle-aged salesman past his prime, she overlooked his thinning hair and the patch of baldness, his expanding girth, and his penchant for cheap food and sloppy eating. He was a sloth. Yet somehow, when he displayed the crooked grin that accentuated the dent in his chin, dialed up the charm and sweetened his glib tongue, he talked his way into many a sale, especially among women customers … as he did her mother.

He didn't really care for kids and told her mother at the onset. Then, he reconsidered as more bright-eyed, younger men came along to join the sales force. He decided a ready-made family with a kid offered him something they didn't have—respectability and social acceptance at another level. So he became a family man, husband and father. To the outside world, he became a responsible member of the community. To Mary Ann, he became her nightmare.

The heavy hand of her stepfather made her wary of men and slow to trust. At first, he was nice, opening car doors for her and her mother, helping them to carry groceries, being a real gentleman. A month into the marriage, his behavior visibly changed with Mary Ann, the kid. He spoke to her gruffly and said hurtful things when they were alone. He was careful not to leave marks or bruises, but he was physically abusive—grabbing her hard, pulling her hair, pushing her, and frightening her. Who knew what he did behind closed doors in the bedroom? Mary Ann wasn't close to her mom and certainly her relationship didn't rise to the level of a confidant. Sometimes at night she heard loud noises, thumping, and shouting.

Mary Ann would concentrate on something else, think of her real father, who died when she was a child. But there were enough memories, good ones, providing anchors in her life.

When she was about four and a half, Mary Ann's father took her to the Christmas tree farm to pick out a live tree. It was cold, the tips of her ears and nose reddened despite the scarf wrapped around her face. Her tiny, mittened hand felt warm and secure, enveloped in the extra-large, gloved hand of her gangly father.

Cheerful Christmas music blared from the wood cabin where they were heading. It was lit with bright, blinking lights and decorated with ornaments hung from the ceiling and fresh wreaths and garlands. The enterprising owner's son, a teenage pimply boy, sold steaming cups of apple cider and hot cocoa from his stand. The mood was festive, with shrieks of laughter, the fresh smell of fir and pine trees, and chirpy notes of holiday tunes floating in the air as Mary Ann happily sipped her hot drink, the warm liquid trickling down her throat.

They would take their time to pick the most beautiful tree. Not the biggest, nor a sapling, but one that was just right. At night, they headed to the fire pit. Mary Ann loved to watch the bonfire, the flames flickering and dancing in the dark. Sitting with her father, she'd stretch her hands toward the fire to warm them. He'd get her a bag of popcorn and ask if she'd want to toast marshmallows. She'd squeal in delight. That was their tradition. He'd put his arms around her shoulders, and she'd snuggle against him. It was perfect, the happiest she'd ever been.

Mary Ann looked up to her father. This was their adventure. Her favorite time of the year. The magical season of Christmas—a special time with him, just the two of them.

She would have one more year like that. Then it would stop. His life was cut tragically short. Nothing was the same after that. A part of her died with him, but she held on to their good memories together.

Chapter 7

WHAT HAD SHE been thinking? It was the holidays. Caught up in the festivities and excitement of the season, but with no one to share it with, Mary Ann was acutely aware of her loneliness. It was at Norma's urging that she had accepted Ron's invite for Christmas. To be fair, he had checked off most of the boxes as she ran down her list quickly in her mind. The list she had memorized. Ron was tall and handsome. A striking and masculine man. Check. Ron was self-sufficient, the owner of the hardware store. Check. He was intelligent. Check. He was single. Check. He was available. Check. He was interested in her. Check. He was friendly. Check. He liked Isabella. *Wait* ... that didn't get a check. Okay, so Ron wasn't a cat person. He preferred dogs. That wasn't a deal breaker ... or was it?

Mary Ann didn't want to be alone for Christmas—or New Year's Eve. Did she use Ron to ease her loneliness? Did she encourage him and lead him on by accepting his invite? Yes, she was selfish. But she'd felt more alone than ever. So much so she couldn't bear to be by herself. So, she went on a date and spent time with Ron. Mary Ann made no promises. They had a good time together, as friends … until the stroke of midnight on New Year's Eve when they kissed.

But it was leading up to that and bound to happen. She'd almost expected it, a wrapping up at the end of the year.

But there were hints along the way, things that sounded alarm bells. Deep within, Mary Ann knew—and her actions betrayed what was in her heart.

She hadn't hung mistletoe on her porch or over her doorway.

She remembered Ron had pressed to come inside her home after their Christmas date, but she didn't invite him in.

There was something else too … something she didn't like. The way Ron poked her in the arm—sharp and hard. The harsh insistence she saw in his eyes instead, when she looked for the warm tenderness of love.

She had brushed aside the warnings that seeped through at first, determined to have a nice holiday with him. What was troubling her … the bits and pieces finally came together, sending chills through her body. Mary Ann suddenly felt weak in her legs and knees, gripping the shower curtain as her body trembled under the warm spray of the morning shower. It was like the wrapping came off—and she saw it clearly for the first time—what was inside, unmistaken in the light of day. She knew the signs so well—her stepfather had taught her.

All along, she felt a guiding hand working behind the

scenes. Maybe it was her father watching out for her? Whatever it was, Mary Ann knew that she wasn't falling in love with Ron—and never would.

Chapter 8

THE NEW YEAR had started with a bang at the flower shop, and then it slowed down. There would be a lull before business started picking up again for Valentine's Day. People who spent too much at Christmas suffered buyers' remorse in the weeks after the holiday rush and gift-buying season passed and things settled down. In the harsh light of the cold wintery days, everything seemed clearer.

After Christmas Eve, Mary Ann had plenty of time to think and replay her conversations with Connor. She convinced herself that in hindsight it was better this way, not to see him again. Otherwise, she sure would give him a piece of her mind, a big piece at that. His invitation for Christmas dinner was a feeble attempt at an apology on his part.

Mary Ann had put Connor out of her mind again, thinking he had gone back to the city after the holidays. The last thing she'd expected was to see Connor in an apron at the market. He was beaming and practically bouncing when he saw her. The excitement was palpable and real.

Intelligent and successful, Connor was also wholesome

and good-looking, though not in a rugged way but more urbane. In the competitive corporate environment, he had relied on his wits, grit, and determination. Luck played a part too—bestowed on this well-dressed, keen young man— in his rise to the coveted office. If anyone added up all of Connor's qualities and talents, it would be impressive.

Maybe it was time she settled down and raised a family? Her clock was ticking, but she had a few more years of eggs ovulating. Still, it was her logical self, thinking.

Should she settle and risk going to her grave with regrets?

Was Mary Ann's heart beating for a certain someone?

Someone who brought out the flush on her cheeks, the fluttering in her belly, the song in her heart, the catch in her throat?

Someone who made her pulse quicken, her steps lighter, and brought a twinkle to her eye?

Dare she hope for more in life, for the grand love of her life—for the person truly worthy of Mary Ann and all she had to offer?

Chapter 9

CONNOR'S GLANCE LINGERED until Mary Ann's figure disappeared. He took a step back, bumping into the rigid surface of the counter. "Ouch," said Connor, putting his hands on his lower back to rub it.

He felt a nudge on his arm.

"You really need to talk to her."

Connor turned, seeing the market's owner. "I tried to, Mrs. Steele."

"When?"

"At the flower shop, after you, all the other customers, and Norma left. We were alone. So … how are you?"

"Young man, when you ask old folks how they are, prepare for a long answer. But I won't bore you with that. I'm as good as I can be," said Mrs. Steele, with a lift in her voice and a firmness that spelled out a no-nonsense and take-charge attitude. She sniffed and shrugged. "You're changing the subject. Did you have a *good* talk back then?"

"Ah, back to that," said Connor. "I apologized to her. Told her how things were after I went back to the city, dealing with my life, my pain. How I went through the motions of living, barely making it through each day."

"Have you told Mary Ann how you felt about her?"

He hesitated. "I told her I've thought of her, picked up the phone and tried to call her." He shook his head and sighed. "But she knows the call never came."

She stared at him. "And then?"

Connor had a feeling that little got by Mrs. Steele. He liked her, despite her quirkiness which he'd glimpsed the first time they had met. But, who was he to judge? People had quirks, all kinds of different ones, and that was one of the things that made everyone different and unique. He liked interesting characters, especially a person who spoke their mind, and she certainly did that. He coughed to clear his throat. Darn, she had a good memory too. He said, "I told Mary Ann I failed poor Tom, too, and I worried about him."

"What did she say?"

"Told me to call Doc Carlson."

"What about today … did you tell her?" she asked quietly.

Connor made no excuses. He straightened and stretched himself to stand tall, chin up.

She focused her sharp blue eyes on him. "You kids *really* need to catch up."

Chapter 10

CONNOR WASN'T USED to such direct questions. He had enough sense to know she demanded a direct answer. No beating around the bush. Maybe she commanded respect because of her age? Or maybe she was always like that, and the trait became more pronounced as she got older. His silence betrayed him, the pause before he answered.

"No, the best intentions can go astray," said Connor.

She frowned. "Well, what went wrong?"

Connor shook his head. "Long story, I'm sure you don't want to hear it."

"Young man, time is what I've got. I'm all ears."

He sighed, thinking about where to begin. She'd probably heard snippets over the years, but not directly from him. He started his story. "I grew up here and left home at eighteen, lured by the big city and eager to start a new life. I went to college, studied hard, and got a good job at the company. Stayed there and worked my way up the ladder to the coveted office with a window," said Connor. He paused, glancing at Mrs. Steele.

"Go on," she said impatiently.

"I was a driven young man, so sure of what I wanted. As the years passed, I came back home to visit less frequently. It was down to twice a year, but I always came back for Christmas and stayed to the New Year," said Connor, speaking softly. "Last year, after my mother passed, I was all alone in this world with no one except for Tom, her cat." His voice quaking now, he paused.

Mrs. Steele reached out, giving him a gentle pat on his arm.

"I … I came back for her funeral. And stayed for three weeks to take care of things. Her husband, my stepfather, had passed first." Connor spoke slowly, at first reluctantly, then with a haste to get it all out to this woman who had strength and a kind, understanding heart beneath her tough, sharp exterior. "I met Mary Ann when she made the flower arrangements for my mother's funeral. I tried to communicate what I wanted and envisioned, and failed miserably at that, or so I thought. She got it, and when I came back to see her arrangement, I saw it was beautiful and perfect for my mother."

A slight smile appeared on Mrs. Steele's face, but she didn't interrupt.

"After the funeral, I bumped into Mary Ann at the grocery store while I was picking up some cat food. She found out about my cat, Tom, and told me about her cat, Isabella. I said, 'Maybe Isabella would like to meet Tom sometime?' Later, I invited her to a dinner I was having at my home with the pastor and his daughter, and Mom's friend and neighbor, Mrs.

Rainer. The dinner was my way of thanking them and honoring my mother." Connor's face lit up as he remembered that warm, cozy evening. "I love to cook, and my mother was the best teacher. That night, we ate, danced to Mom's favorite records, and watched the cats play." He paused, reflectively. "I felt Mom was there … and I wasn't all alone."

"She probably was," said Mrs. Steele, her voice soft and kind.

"I spent more time with Mary Ann, and we went out to dinner before I left. We had a delicious Italian meal. We talked and got to know each other better. But my time here was ending—I had used up the three weeks off work I took for the funeral and to put things in order. I left the next day and returned to the city."

Connor ran his fingers through his hair. He pursed his lips. Mad at himself at what he did next, or rather—what he didn't do.

"For the next four months or so, I barely survived, going through the motions at work and neglecting Tom. I didn't call Mary Ann. Didn't want to be a burden to her, or use her as a crutch. But I found out differently when I came back in town, the day before Christmas Eve." Connor stared at the old woman, owning up to it. "I had hurt her by not calling, leaving her like that."

"What are you going to do about it?" said Mrs. Steele.

"Do? I can't force her to give me another chance."

"Do you want to win her back?"

Connor was taken aback by her directness. "*Win …* *her*—"

She nodded.

"I messed up, okay?" He gritted his teeth.

"Young man—"

"Yes," sighed Connor, his chin quivering. He withstood her unwavering glance even as she waited. *He wanted Mary Ann. But could he admit that, out loud, to Mrs. Steele—and to himself?*

She said, "You know what to do."

Chapter 11

AFTER MRS. STEELE made her way down the aisle, Connor occupied himself with busy work, cleaning up and wiping a spill on the countertop. At the end of the counter he noticed a carton of soup, sitting where Mary Ann had left it. *Had she forgotten it in her hurry to leave?* He picked it up and popped off the lid to check. It was the chili. *Her chili.* His heart thumped, beating faster. *I could bring it to her*, he thought.

Connor whipped off his apron and dashed back into the kitchen, holding on to her soup. He shouted to the cook, "We closing early man, I'm taking off." He grabbed his jacket and rushed toward the cash register. When it was his turn, he paid for the chili, putting rubber bands around the carton and over the lid to secure it before placing it carefully in doubled-paper bags.

A burst of cold wind blasted his face as he opened the door, whirling flurries of snow greeting him. He headed for the flower shop, farther down on Main Street. The sidewalk was already slick, wet, and covered by a dusting of snow as he arrived in front of Mary Ann's store. A handwritten display in the window confirmed he was too late, and beyond it the darkened interior. Seeing the "Closed" sign on the door, he cursed. He'd just missed her. He stood on the sidewalk as people hastened by, scurrying to rush home, not one person strolling or stopping to talk.

Holding the bag, Connor pondered what to do next. There was only one thing he could do—his pulse raced with excitement and he shuddered with uncertainty. He wanted to see her again, and this could be another opportunity. He could drop off Mary Ann's soup at her home. He'd never been there, but they had exchanged contact information four months ago. Taking out his cell phone, Connor quickly scrolled to her name and found her address.

The drive to her home was short, only a few minutes. As Connor arrived at her place, he recognized her car parked outside. His heart raced as he moved quickly, before he lost his nerve and chickened out. In quick succession, he slid out, locked his SUV, and walked up to her door. He knocked once, then two quick taps. He waited. Counting the seconds, he hesitated, wondering if he'd made the right decision. Would he have time to make it back to his car and drive away before she came to the door? Shuffling his feet, he made a move to step away—just as the door swung open.

"Why Connor," said Mary Ann. Her eyes widened and a flush of red appeared on her cheeks.

"Uh, I—" said Connor, glancing down as Isabella greeted him with a meow, her body rubbing against the legs of his jeans. He chuckled, giving a silent prayer of thanks for this perfectly timed break, and searched for the right words.

"Isabella likes you. She doesn't do this to everybody," said Mary Ann.

A sheepish grin spread slowly across his face. "I like her, and I'm sure Tom does too."

Mary Ann shivered as splats of wet snowflakes landed on her bare arm. "Well, don't just stand there, come in." She giggled, adding, "I won't bite."

Connor stepped across the doorstep. Her home was warm and cheery inside. It was modest. A few attractive pieces of modern furniture, some tasteful decorations, and small glass vases of bright flowers adorned the living room. He wiped his feet on the doormat, stomping to release the snow.

"I just got here a few minutes ago," said Mary Ann, closing the door behind him.

"Here's your soup," said Connor, handing her the paper bag.

"Oh, thanks! I realized I'd left it at the market when I put away the groceries. I'm sorry you had to go to the trouble."

"No trouble at all. I was about to leave and noticed it on the counter. I'm afraid it's gotten cold by now."

"I'll just warm it up," said Mary Ann. She took the package from him and whipped off the paper bags, seeing the round paper carton. She plucked off the rubber bands and headed to the kitchen.

At that moment, Connor's stomach growled. He clasped his chest, as if his lungs had anything to do with his belly.

Mary Ann glanced back, lips twitching as they betrayed a smile.

"Well … uh … I best be going," mumbled Connor as he turned to leave.

Chapter 12

LEAVING SO SOON? Looking at Connor, the ill feelings Mary Ann had harbored in her heart were no longer at the forefront. Empathy crept in, and a flutter of regret. Was he just here to do his job, making sure she got her soup? She turned away as tears pricked her eyes. She quickly put the soup container down and snatched a tissue from a box on the kitchen counter. She prayed he didn't glimpse the wet gleam on her cheeks. She didn't trust herself to speak until she cleared the lump from her throat.

When she'd composed herself, she realized that Connor was still standing by the door. He had an odd look on his face, sort of contorted, like he was trying to hold his stomach in— or something else.

"You're not ill, are you?" Mary Ann walked toward him.

He shook his head. Then his stomach sounded again. No mistaking it, and this time it was a louder, deeper rumble. The funny look on Connor's face was priceless as his arms crossed over his tummy.

"You're sure?" she teased, dragging out the moment.

He mumbled as he spoke, so low she couldn't catch any words.

She saw his eyes, darting around as if to escape, and burst out laughing. Mary Ann released her pent-up anger and negative emotions, expelling them, as the weight lifted.

Chapter 13

MARY ANN WAS holding her hands over her face, gasping before giggles burst out of her lips again.

Relieved and finding the perfect moment to cover his embarrassment, Connor broke out with laughter of his own.

The only one who had a straight face was Isabella. Connor glimpsed the cat, reclining quietly in the corner, observing the two humans making a racket. One of her ears was flicked back at an odd angle. Connor hooted as he pointed at Isabella, urging Mary Ann to look. All the while her cat remained composed, regal, a slight quiver of whiskers betraying her vexed tolerance of the silly humans.

When Mary Ann finally recovered, she straightened and walked back to the kitchen. "I've just made a fresh pot of coffee." She grabbed two mugs. "The least I could do is offer you a cup and a bite to eat, you know … to quell the rumbling."

"Yes," said Connor. His legs carried him across the room in swift strides before she changed her mind.

"Cream and sugar?"

"Black for me, please."

"We can share the soup," said Mary Ann as she popped the cardboard carton in the microwave. She opened the refrigerator and pulled out a block of cheese, quickly slicing it and arranging the pieces on a plate, adding the freshly baked French bread she had just purchased in the market. She placed a cluster of grapes in the middle. Holding the plate in one hand and her coffee mug in the other, she nodded to Connor, tilting her head toward the dining room table.

Connor grabbed two bowls and spoons, the soup carton, and his mug. As he passed Isabella, he gave her a wink.

Chapter 14

AFTER THE LAST drop of coffee was gone, the soup consumed, and the plate of bread and cheese cleaned up, they still sat at the table and talked, getting to know each other again. Tossing shy, flirtatious glances between the laughs and giggles.

Connor didn't want to move, but from where he sat, he could see the fading sunlight and the nonstop flurries outside the window. He yearned for spring to come soon, and with it, the blossoming of flowers and love in the air.

He slowly pushed back his chair and stood up, gathering the empty plate and bowls, and mugs and spoons, taking them to the kitchen.

"Just leave them in the sink," said Mary Ann, hearing the clinking of dishes as he set them down.

"Okay," said Connor. He picked up his jacket, put it on and zipped it closed. Opening the door, he peered outside. A layer of soft snow blanketed the ground. His foot rested on the doorstep. He paused, his fingers jiggling the car keys as he delayed his departure for a few more seconds. He turned to Mary Ann, giving a broad grin. "Listen, I had a great time." He wanted to hug Mary Ann. But all he managed to say as he headed out the door was a "thank you."

Connor had parked his SUV right in front, next to Mary Ann's car. He cleared the snow from the windshield, windows, and hood before he got inside and turned the key. It didn't crank. He tried again. The engine didn't turn over. It was dead. His eyes met Mary Ann through the windshield.

She dashed outside to his car as he rolled down the window. "Got jumper cables?"

"In the trunk," said Connor, getting out. He opened the trunk, grabbed the cables, and popped his hood open.

Mary Ann ran back inside to grab her car keys and returned, clasping her sweater tightly as a blast of cold wind blew, stinging her uncovered face. She popped her hood and waited until Connor connected the cables before she started her car.

"Pump it," yelled Connor.

She pressed her foot on the gas pedal, giving it a few hard taps.

Connor tried again to start his car. Only the still sound of a dead crank met his ears.

Mary Ann rolled down her window. "We can call the guy from the garage. He has a tow truck."

Connor turned off his key and got out of his car. He was ashamed to admit that he had neglected his car in the last few months. He stood there, muttering under his breath, oblivious to the mass of swirling snowflakes landing on his head, melting into his hair.

"Come on, let's go inside and call him," she said as she moved back toward the front door.

Connor shivered as a gust of cold air slammed his face. He followed her to the door, again stomping the snow from his shoes before going inside.

Mary Ann removed the phone book from a kitchen drawer and put it on the counter, flipping it open to the auto repair section.

Pulling out his cell phone, Connor quickly dialed the number for the garage. There was no answer. After four rings, it went to voice mail. He left his name and cell, and her home phone number, with a brief message about the problem. "I'll try again if he doesn't call back soon."

She nodded, setting the phone book back in the drawer.

He started to put away his phone, but changed his mind and dialed another number. It was picked up after one ring. "Mrs. Rainer? This is Connor."

Mary Ann listened as Connor explained what happened. He asked Mrs. Rainer for a favor, to check in on Tom and feed him.

He ended the call, then filled her in on it. "Mrs. Rainer still has the key to Mom's house, and she'll take care of Tom." He let out a long breath, relieved that she'd agreed to help.

"Give me your wet jacket," said Mary Ann in a firm voice. She walked away and hung it on the coat rack to dry. "There's nothing else you can do now."

"I hope the guy calls soon."

"You mean Clay—"

"Yeah, is he reliable?"

"He's helped me out and Norma, too. However, it may be a while since he's busy, especially in this weather."

Chapter 15

IN NO TIME at all, they found themselves back at the dining room table. Connor put his cell phone on the table where he could see it. He almost jumped when the phone buzzed. He put it on speakerphone when the phone number of the tow truck guy flashed. "Hello?"

"Hey, it's Clay calling you back. So, what's wrong with your car?" said the man on the other end. He sounded rushed.

"My car won't start. Can you give me a tow?"

"I'm swamped. I can't come to you anytime soon."

"What's your best estimate?"

"Can't say."

Connor choked. "It's *that* bad out there?"

"Let's put it this way. I may head home myself before the missus gets real mad."

"I don't blame you. Stay safe. Thanks, man," said Connor, ending the call.

Mary Ann threw him a sympathetic glance. "There's nothing you can do till he gets here."

"It sounded like I may be in for a long wait," said

Connor, frowning. He ran his fingers through his hair and massaged the tense muscles in his neck.

"Might as well relax."

"What do you do to relax?"

"Oh, I read books, listen to music, watch a good movie," said Mary Ann, maintaining a calm, soothing voice.

"Got any cards … normal cards with a king, queen, and a joker?"

Mary Ann pushed her chair back and stood up. "I may have one stashed away in the closet. I brought a box of games and stuff when I moved here, and I'm pretty sure there's a deck of cards shoved in there." She left for a few minutes and reappeared with a triumphant grin, holding a box of cards in her raised hand like she won a trophy.

Connor smiled. "So, how about playing some card games?"

She shrugged, raising her eyebrows. "I haven't played in a long while."

Connor took the deck from her, opening the box. His fingers glided over the slippery, waxy texture, loving the feel of new cards. His hands moved like a choreographed dance—a tap on the table, a flick of the wrist—making a quick cut, shuffling, and the ruffling of cards.

Staring at his long fingers, deftly dealing the cards, Mary Ann was mesmerized. Like a child being shown a magic trick, watching every move, not wanting to miss any action.

"Know how to play Old Maid?" asked Connor.

She shook her head.

"Hearts … Rummy?"

"Nope."

"Ever play Go Fish?"

"It's been awhile," said Mary Ann. "I'll need a refresher."

Connor explained the game and Mary Ann nodded, listening.

"Oh, if the card you draw from the stack is the card you asked for, then you get another turn to draw."

"So how do you win?" Her eyes widened, innocent and inquisitive.

Connor liked Mary Ann's childlike curiosity, her willingness to learn new things, to figure it out. "When you get a book of four cards of one kind, you place it on the table, face up. The player with the most books wins. A game ends when all the cards are played and books are displayed on the table." Connor grinned. "See how easy it is?"

They bantered back and forth. She used her novice status to real advantage, asking more and more questions. As the game warmed up, it went faster. Mary Ann squealed in delight when she won anything. It was so silly, and Connor laughed so hard.

He'd never seen this side of her. It jogged his fond memories of his childhood and his parents, so long ago. How much time they'd spent on the crossword puzzles in the newspaper. His dad sitting on the oversized reclining chair in the living room, wearing his short-sleeve cotton shirt, reading glasses hanging low over his nose, the newspaper flipped to the crossword puzzle. His mom propping on the armrest and leaning over his shoulder, her slender finger pointing to a word he'd thoughtfully filled in as she whispered something in his ear, the gray strands of her hair loose, falling over her face, her hand touching his arm affectionately. The adoring glances his dad gave her.

There were playful times too, when his dad was focused on his crossword puzzle, all serious and frowning, and she'd tried to get his attention. Running her finger down his cheek, tugging or tweaking his ear, ruffling his hair, or wiggling the eyeglasses dangling on the edge of his nose. But he wouldn't get mad at her. Connor waited for him to swat her hand away like a mosquito. The first time his mom did it, he clutched her hand, still keeping his eyes on the puzzle. After that, she'd try again. He'd turn his head slightly and kiss her hand, then let it go. Other times, he'd look at her and say, "Mabel, I need to concentrate on this," telling her he didn't want to be interrupted, his voice soft-spoken yet firm, commanding her respect.

Connor sat back and watched Mary Ann, playing like a pro. A real pro. He'd ask if she had a card, just because he was holding one. She'd shake her head. Later, when he almost thought she'd forgotten, she'd come back around and she'd get him, claiming his card. Connor was good-natured and laughed. All Connor wanted to do was relax and have some fun. If he won, that was fine.

But he wasn't focused *just* on winning … *the cards, that is.*

Chapter 16

HE LOST ALL track of time, but a glance at the darkened sky outside told Connor it was late. His cell phone stayed where it was on the table, untouched since the last call. A yawn escaped as Connor's hand fumbled toward his coffee mug.

Mary Ann raised her eyebrows, glancing up from her cards. "I'm on a roll."

He raised the mug to his lips, catching the last drop. "That's it," said Connor as he slowly set it down.

Mary Ann snatched the last card from the stack and beamed in triumph as she slapped the last four-card book down. She counted out loud. "Eight, I win."

"What?" Connor mumbled. It'd been a long day, and his mind was operating on its last battery.

"Aren't you going to write the score?" She paused, waiting for him to tally it.

He rubbed his face, pulling the skin down over his cheeks, then blinked his weary eyes. It took a moment before it sunk in, what she had asked, before he picked up the pencil and scribbled the number on the pad. He dropped the pencil, and it bounced, making a soft plop as it landed across the table and rolled to a stop. "What time is it?"

"About eleven-thirty."

He yawned, covering his mouth, and stood up to stretch, struggling to keep awake. "Well, I need to get going."

"But … your car."

"Oh, yeah," murmured Connor. He was so tired he'd forgotten about his car. All he wanted to do now was sleep. "Clay … he didn't call."

"He won't come this late," said Mary Ann.

"I should go." Connor fumbled with his shirt, straightening out the sleeves. Checking the buttons. He had fun tonight, hanging out with her, playing the card game. Man, was he wiped out.

From the look on her face, he thought Mary Ann seemed disappointed. Was it because the game ended? Or because he was leaving? But wait—wasn't he stranded? He didn't want to go anywhere, and he couldn't. He was too much of a gentleman to ask her for help, to impose on her anymore. If he had to, he'd sleep on the floor.

"You'd best stay here." Mary Ann stood up and walked to the hall closet, pulling out a thick folded blanket and a pillow. "You can crash on the couch tonight. I doubt Clay will show up at this hour."

"I—I don't know." He mumbled, smiling shyly.

"Here, take it," said Mary Ann.

Connor reached out to grab the plaid blanket and pillow, swaying a bit as weariness descended. His fingers slipped and brushed across her hand. It was small and soft. He felt a zing, a spark of electricity as they touched.

He stared at her. Did she feel it too? He thought so, from the flicker of surprise that flashed across her face.

Connor felt a small surge of adrenaline, a crazy overwhelming desire to wrap Mary Ann inside the blanket as she stood near him. He pictured her in it—the soft cotton of the red plaid framing her lovely face. He could purchase another one for a matching set, but it must be a blue plaid blanket. He smiled to himself as he recalled a day long ago in his bedroom when he threw a fit at his mother, shouting in his childish voice that he must have a room painted blue.

He wrestled with his emotions. He could just casually whip the blanket around her; perhaps make a joke about it, like it's big enough for two. But Connor also wanted to do nothing more than sleep. He was losing it. Tiredness won out. He grabbed the pillow and tossed it on the end of the couch. He kicked off his shoes before he sunk onto the white couch.

"Good night," Connor muttered, glimpsing the red plaid color as he pulled the blanket over him and surrendered to sleep, his eyelids fluttering shut. In his dreams Mrs. Steele poked him, her blue eyes piercing. He could hear her voice chanting, *"Win her back—"*

Chapter 17

MARY ANN CLOSED her bedroom door, took off her clothes, and pulled on her long underwear. She slid between the cool sheets and snuggled under the thick fluffy comforter.

Easing one shoulder and wiggling into a comfortable position to settle in for the night, she took care not to disturb the familiar bump of the small warm body curled next to her. She cocked her head to look at Isabella, already checked out in la-la land.

She thought back to the day's events—running into Connor in the market, forgetting her soup, and rushing to get home before the storm. She hadn't expected Connor to deliver her soup in person—nor his car trouble. She had fun playing card games. Mary Ann saw a side of Connor that she hadn't before—a playful, easygoing, lighthearted side. *Who would have thought he had a sense of humor?* She had responded, giggling like a schoolgirl, flirting innocently with him. She had thoroughly enjoyed it. And, then … the touch of his fingers on the back of her hand.

She fell asleep with a smile on her lips.

Chapter 18

CONNOR WOKE UP to bright light streaming in the window. He didn't expect he'd sleep so soundly, descending into a deep, dream-filled realm. Connor stretched, his mind groggy, taking a second to realize where he was: not the familiar blue walls of his bedroom, but the beige walls of a strange room. He bolted to a sitting position, viewing his surroundings. Then it came back to him … the plaid blanket, the white couch, the cards on the dining room table. He looked down the hallway. The door to Mary's Ann room was closed. It was quiet. He swung his legs off the couch and got up.

During the night, the storm had raged, dropping a ton of snow. He opened the curtains of the living room window and touched the icy cold glass pane; the frost clinging to it. The world had transformed into a white landscape. The wind had retreated, leaving behind a stillness and frigid cold. Connor shivered. He padded to the kitchen in his socks to make coffee, filling fresh water in the coffee maker. He opened the refrigerator door, whistling when he saw the shelves well-stocked with food. Intent on checking out the contents, he didn't hear Mary Ann until she walked up to him in her fluffy slippers.

"Good morning," said Mary Ann, cheerfully. She wore a long-sleeved cotton top and loose pants; her hair was tied up in a ponytail.

"You're perky this early?" He looked at her face, freshly scrubbed and natural.

She nodded. "I slept well. Did you?"

"Your couch wasn't so bad. My back isn't hurting." Connor grinned, pivoting his shoulders and stretching his back.

Isabella chose this moment to approach her food bowl, strutting her way to the kitchen with her tail curled up in the air.

Mary Ann reached down to pet Isabella's back and scratch behind her ears. "And you slept well on my bed." She picked up the cat's empty bowls and washed them before pouring fresh dry food in one bowl and water in the other.

"What can I do?" Connor asked.

"Feed me quick," said Mary Ann, smiling. Making a funny face.

"Scrambled eggs and toast coming right up," said Connor, reaching for the carton of eggs and rummaging in the fridge. "Where's your butter?"

"The soft butter in the tub is on the top shelf to the right. There should also be a couple of sticks in the butter compartment in the refrigerator door."

Connor had the skillet heating on low while he cracked

eggs on the edge of the bowl and beat eggs, milk, salt and pepper with a whisk. A delicious aroma burst out as he slid a generous slab of creamy butter in the frying pan and poured in the egg mixture, making slow scrambled eggs. While it was cooking, he popped two slices of bread in the toaster.

Mary Ann filled two glasses with orange juice and brought them to the dining room table, putting them down next to the steaming cups of coffee.

In no time at all, breakfast was on the table. Sitting across from Mary Ann as the bright sunlight streamed in the windows and cast a pleasant glow on her face, Connor couldn't help but think how much he was enjoying this. After years of being single and eating alone at home, it was nice to just relax and enjoy a meal with someone. He thought he knew what he wanted. But now he wanted more—with Mary Ann—and the joys of having breakfast for two was just the beginning.

Maybe it was the angle of the light, thought Connor, as he looked into her eyes, shining bright—and perhaps there was a glint of affection. His heartbeat quickened at the thought, bringing with it a sliver of hope. Her eyes seemed different this sunny morning, after last night. He wouldn't ask the question that had been eating at him for so long or press her for an answer until she had her breakfast and coffee.

"Have patience", his mother would say when he was a little boy, when he couldn't contain his excitement at Christmas. His eyes had bulged at the sight of the colorful, decked-out fir tree in their living room and the pile of wrapped presents underneath. He would rip off the gift wrap, not caring how it tore. His mother, though, took her time to unwrap each gift. They had a tradition of opening one present at a time, each person taking a turn. He didn't know what was worse, the waiting for his own gifts, or the waiting for her to open hers. But he knew she loved him, for all his faults and foibles, for all the troubles he got into growing up and the pain he caused. His mother never lashed out at him. It took him a long time to understand this and put himself into her shoes. How she put up with him was beyond Connor.

He wanted to be the man he wasn't for his mother. Connor wanted to show Mary Ann he could learn from his mistakes and do it over, and better. His mother would have given him second chances, but she was gone now. He'd like to believe she was still there, in spirit, and watching over him. A tiny flame of love fanned in his heart—a heart that held on to hope.

Connor watched Mary Ann as she ate, the way she held her fork, the dainty bites she took. He knew she must have been famished, but she didn't throw away her manners.

This morning he saw her face, bare and without makeup. Mary Ann looked beautiful, youthful, and vibrant.

Connor raked his fingers through his hair. Was Mary Ann so comfortable around him she didn't bother with makeup? Or did she think of him as just a friend crashing on the couch—nothing more?

He took a long, deep breath, as he watched Mary Ann take the last bite of food on her plate. "Finished?"

She put the fork down on her plate and dabbed her mouth with a napkin, covering the broad grin underneath. "All done."

"Good?"

"Yummy! Oh my gosh, it's *the best* scrambled eggs I've ever had, Connor."

"That is *the best* compliment I've ever gotten," he said, giving her a thumbs-up. He felt like singing, shouting to the world. He wanted to bask in her praise and soak it in, while another part of him flinched, glitzy with excitement. "You can dress it up with cream or cheese, or sprinkle toppings on it," Connor added, keeping his voice calm and steady while his heart raced.

He got up to take her plate and clear the table. "I'll do the dishes." Noticing her near-empty cup of coffee, he made a mental note to bring back a refill before sitting down to have "the talk" with Mary Ann. He could see Mrs. Steele now and hear her stern voice saying, "Do you want to win her back?"

Chapter 19

THE PHONE RANG, but Connor couldn't hear what Mary Ann was saying. The sound of the running water in the sink muffled her words. His thoughts had dwelled on the moment—the big moment he'd been dreaming of, choosing with care the words he'd say to her. He rolled them over in his mind, syllable by syllable, running with it, then reworking it, and rehearsing it. He imagined how she'd respond: perhaps a kiss or the moist glint in her eyes as she teared up when he finally declared the secret in his heart. His love. Connor hastened to finish washing the dishes and cut the water off, catching the last part of her conversation.

"I'm all right," said Mary Ann. She paused. "Yes, quite sure. Clay gave you the address, but he couldn't come, so you're helping?"

Connor could see her shaking her head from side to side.

"So, you thought it was me when you realized where it was … no, it's not my car," said Mary Ann, as she lifted her eyebrow and shot a glance his way across the room. "It's my friend's car."

She dropped her voice and mumbled into the phone, cupping one hand over her mouth. "Okay, see you soon."

"I overheard. Help is on the way?" asked Connor.

"Your car's going to get towed."

Connor managed a weak smile as he looked away. It was too soon to leave. Everything had been perfect this morning. Breakfast was barely over, and now this—his hopes were dashed again just as he was working up the nerve to tell her how he felt. Would he get another chance?

He was expecting the knock on the door. Still, he jumped at the sound.

Mary Ann opened the door. The sound of her voice, clear and welcoming, as if she was greeting an old friend.

He heard a murmur, a masculine voice. Long arms reaching out to embrace Mary Ann, large, lean, strong hands protruding from the sleeves clasped around her back.

A sinking feeling grabbed Connor, seeing the man's arms wrapped around her. A coldness seized his heart, seeping into it. The embrace—was there a possessiveness, a familiarity? The warm blood pumping in his arteries turned to an iciness, slowing his heart, spreading throughout his body with each heartbeat. The pumping sound of his heart dimmed to a slow beat, crawling, almost frozen in space. Was he too late?

She pulled back and glanced at Connor standing in the living room, his jacket already on. "He's here. Let's go."

Connor gripped the pull on the zipper, tugging it as he pulled it closed, and strode across the living room, keys in one hand, expecting to meet the tow-truck guy or someone from the repair shop. But the guy *wasn't* a stranger.

"Ron," said Connor, stopped in his tracks.

Ron flinched, doing a double take. Recovering quickly, he let go of Mary Ann and grabbed Connor's shoulders, then shook his hand. "Didn't expect to see you here."

Thoughts whirled in Connor's mind as muscles tightened around his throat. What was he doing here? But most of all, he wanted to know why Ron had his arms wrapped around Mary Ann.

"You're back?" asked Ron.

"Yup."

"For good?"

"I left the city and moved back."

Ron squinted and took a step back. "I thought you'd take up my offer to partner with me on my hardware store."

"Your offer was generous, and I wrestled with the decision. But, like I said to you, thank you, but I can't accept."

"You had months to think about it," Ron persisted, irritation coming across in his voice.

"I'm sorry for taking so long to respond." Pulling his head back, Connor gave a slight shake. "I came back, but it wasn't for that."

Chapter 20

TUGGING OFF HIS gloves, Connor glanced at Ron sitting beside him, driving the tow truck with his SUV in the back. The crunch of tires in the snow was the only sound. The silence stretched as Connor looked out the frost-coated passenger side window, his breathing fogging the glass. The snowy landscape whirled by in a mass of white, broken by the contrasting stark darkness of trees, partially coated with thick layers of snow. Icicles hung from the exposed branches like icy daggers.

A cold stillness replaced the fury of yesterday's blowing wind. He could see the frozen beauty of the wintry day. In the silence of the truck's cab, Connor reflected on his friendship with Ron. He remembered, as kids, the silly pranks they had played, the scrapes and troubles they had gotten into, and out of, together. The fun times they'd had. He took a deep breath and broke the silence.

"Hey Ron, thanks for the tow. How's Clay?"

"Clay worked so hard yesterday he wore himself out. He called me this morning and asked me to help."

"Last night I talked to him, it sounded like he was swamped," said Connor.

"You stayed overnight at Mary Ann's house?" Ron asked, changing the subject.

"Yep, my car wouldn't start."

"How did you two meet?"

"I met her at the flower shop when I came back to town. She made the floral arrangements for my mother's funeral." Connor bristled at the questions. But he kept his tone even.

"Are the two of you just friends?" asked Ron, casually. His hands tightened their grip on the wheel.

"She's the best florist I know," said Connor. "After the funeral, I got to know her better, so yes, I'd say we are friends. Why are you asking?" This line of questioning was getting personal. He threw his question back at Ron.

Ron didn't answer right away. He clenched his teeth and pressed his lips, staring straight ahead at the road. "We've been dating."

Dating? Connor's thoughts came to a full stop. He didn't see this coming. He choked back a gasp, touching his throat. Was this the reason Mary Ann didn't accept his invitation for Christmas supper? He opened his mouth to say something, but all he managed was a raspy repeat of the word, "Dating—"

Hiding a cocky half-smile, Ron kept his eyes on the road and nodded.

Connor's shoulders sagged as he looked down, twisting the gloves in his hands. *Was he too late?* The thought of losing Mary Ann brought a heaviness he couldn't shake off. Hope had sustained him in the months of grief after his mother's death—in moments of dark despair when his heart ached in deep places it had never sunk to before, when the loss and pain was unbearable, when he came face-to-face with the stark loneliness of being all alone in this world.

He shivered, tightening the scarf around his neck.

Chapter 21

A SINKING SENSATION descended in Mary Ann's stomach when the tow truck pulled away.

She had listened to the exchange between the two men. How could she have been so wrong? She had incorrectly assumed Ron's offer of partnership was the *real* reason Connor had come back into town—a business deal. But he had turned Ron down. Connor said he didn't come back for that … so why did he? She had surmised he wasn't interested in her.

Mary Ann's mouth suddenly felt dry. She pictured the two of them riding in the tow truck. Would Ron mention they had dated, that she spent Christmas with him instead? How would Connor react when he found out about it? How was she to know Connor would come back to stay? If it wasn't for a business partnership with Ron, then Connor moved back to his hometown for another reason. It had been a surprise to her too.

Connor had often appeared in her thoughts out of the blue. It didn't matter what she was doing. He'd pop up at odd times and places: when Mary Ann was taking a shower, doing the dishes, reading, walking. Out of nowhere. It put a smile to her lips.

She had felt renewed as she flipped the new calendar to January. What would this new year bring? Although Mary Ann hadn't made resolutions in recent years, she had felt inspired to make one this year.

Hope had seeped into her heart—new thoughts and feelings put a spring in her steps and a song in her heart. She wasn't a mushy kind of girl, but always the sensible, calm one. It was unlike her to live her life this way. She kept this newness within her, not telling anyone, giving it time to grow, like a seed newly sprouted.

Once, years ago, she had been the object of a crush. A boy in school had followed her all year, leaving her little notes but never signing them. However, it wasn't hard to figure out who it was. She felt pleased at first, but then it got irritating, like a buzzing gnat circling around her, not leaving her alone. She tried to be polite to the boy, throwing him an occasional smile out of pity, which only seemed to encourage him. He got bolder, writing longer notes, leaving them on her desk or slipping them through the cracks in her locker. Once he even bumped into her in the hallway. When she dropped her books, he picked them up. As he handed them to her, his hands touched hers. She was sure he did it on purpose. When they touched, she felt nothing. No sparks, no tingling, nothing.

Eventually, he tired of it. But it took months.

This thing, with Ron, was nothing like that. He was a grown man, tall, muscular, and smart. She liked that combination. Her equal. Oh, and did she forget handsome? A list-topper. At first glance, he had the most wonderful qualities and other talents. She told herself there was a reason why tall, dark, and handsome fit the bill.

Ron had called her every day between Christmas and New Year's Eve. They talked, quickly if it was during the day, longer in the evening. They had dinner together two times that week. The first time in a restaurant she had picked. Ron was hopeless in the kitchen, and he'd only get in the way. Mary Ann tried to teach him how to make spaghetti once, and he even messed that up. She didn't mind cooking, since it was fun for her. But cooking for one was certainly not as much fun as for two. Not counting her cat, Isabella, that is. Besides, Isabella's taste buds resided strictly within cat food, and she had the most discriminating tastes for certain particularly tasty, and expensive, brands.

Mary Ann had built up this thing with Ron in her mind, fitting him into a desired slot, filling an empty void made even more pressing because of the holidays. He checked most of her boxes. *Most, but not all.* The kiss on New Year's Eve betrayed what was, or rather, what *wasn't* in her heart of hearts. Boosted by the desire for love and a connection in the holiday season, Mary Ann had lost herself before coming face-to-face with the truth. There was no depth, no spark. The superficial connection fizzled.

Mary Ann closed the door to her home. Alone with Isabella.

Chapter 22

CONNOR WENT STRAIGHT to Mrs. Rainer's home after Ron dropped him off, leaving his towed car at Clay's garage.

"You're here," said Alana as she opened the door, a wide grin splashed across her face as she greeted him warmly.

"I came by to let you guys know and pick up Tom," said Connor. He averted his eyes, looking downward.

"How's your car? Come in and tell me what happened."

Connor didn't look like his usual self. Alana kept the worry out of her voice. He was her friend, and she was determined to find out what went wrong, if it was his car or if it was something else.

Alana tugged his arm, pulling him inside. "You look like you need a warm cup of coffee. I've got a fresh pot, and I'm not taking 'no' for an answer."

As the door closed behind him, Connor heard the crackles from the fireplace and saw the bright flames dancing. Tom was curled up on a rug on the floor in front of the fire, sleeping.

"Let me hang this up," said Alana, as Connor shrugged

off his jacket. "You can sit on the sofa and get warmed up while I get the coffee. Mom's in her room taking a nap, but I'm sure she'll be delighted to see you when she wakes up."

The faint odor of fresh paint lingered in the air, and Connor noticed the drop cloth flung on top of the closed paint bucket lid in the hallway. Alana had replaced the dull gray somber–looking walls with new colors in the living room, livening it up and bringing warmth and comfort to the home she now shared with her mother. This was her labor of love when she returned home on Christmas Eve.

"It looks amazing—you've given it a face-lift," said Connor.

"When I finished the living room after Christmas, Mom loved it so much she wanted me to paint the rest of the rooms," said Alana. She handed Connor a mug of steaming coffee and sat down beside him.

"You got yourself a big project."

"We went together to pick out the paint color at the hardware store. You should've seen Mom, how excited she was. The dull gray in her room needed to go."

"What color did she pick?"

"It's a toss between the white or another shade of gray. I told her to try beige and pick the shade she wanted for paint color."

Connor raised his eyebrows. "And?"

"I was half-joking, expecting her to pick the pale gray that was closer to the gray in her room now, but she's considering the other one I suggested."

"At least she didn't go for bright red," Connor said.

Alana rolled her eyes, laughing. "It'll be pretty. I'll pick up more paint tomorrow. It keeps me busy."

"Are you going to change the color in your bedroom?"

"I've got mine picked out. It's a light, airy shade of blue-green. I think Mom may go with a classic beige, which goes well with her rustic wood furniture and the wooden floors."

"If you need help, just holler. I'm next door." Connor chuckled.

"I may take you up on that."

Connor sat back on the comfy sofa. It was old, the fabric faded, and his body slid into the concave depression in the cushioned seat. Connor's tense muscles relaxed as he sipped the coffee, the warm liquid making its way to his belly. The heat from the fireplace warmed his fingers and toes. Dottie's place felt more like a home now, but it hadn't been that way for years.

After her husband had died and Alana left, Dottie's heart was broken. She had let this place go, and her home fell into disrepair. No longer inviting, it became cold and dark. Dottie would visit Connor's mom next door. When Connor came home during the holidays, Dottie would be there. She was like family—she had no one, and they were the only family she had.

He felt a gentle touch on his arm. Alana leaned in, peering intently into his eyes.

Connor took a deep breath, reminded once more of his troubles.

"How's your car?" asked Alana.

"It got towed to the service station."

"You're not hurt or anything?"

Connor shook his head.

"What's wrong?" A frown furrowed Alana's smooth face. "Look, I'm here if you want to talk about it."

"I—"

"We've both gone through so much pain." Alana squeezed Connor's arm gently.

Connor bowed his head, feeling the sadness in his heart.

She said, "I'm sorry about your mom. I miss my dad, too. It's been years, but I still cry."

"I'm sorry about your dad, too."

"I have a hard time on anniversaries, especially the day he died, and on holidays—Father's Day and Christmas."

"I miss my mom … just talking about her." Connor wiped away a tear as he choked up.

"You know what I do when I'm feeling that way?"

Connor looked up.

"I keep memories of my dad—of us together. Happy memories," said Alana. She touched her chest. "My birthdays, the fun times we had together. The time I found an inchworm crawling on the ground." Her voice cracked as her eyes stared into space, remembering. "It was this thin, green thing. It crawled, arching in the middle. I had never seen an inchworm before. It fascinated me. My dad used it to encourage learning. We made a trip to the library and looked up interesting facts about the inchworm, its life cycle and its habitat."

"I'm glad you shared that story with me," said Connor. "You're not kidding with me, right? About the inchworm."

"No, I'll never look at an inchworm the same way again," said Alana, her eyes crinkling as a smile crept up.

"I've been thinking of doing something to honor my mother," said Connor.

Alana sat up, alert. "She'd like that. What do you have in mind?"

"You know she had a lot of recipes. I'm going through them and creating new ones inspired by her. I'd like to publish a cookbook and dedicate it to the memory of my mother."

"Ooh," squealed Alana, clapping. "I can help you with that, and I think my mom would like to take part too."

Connor hadn't thought of asking for help, but it seemed like a great idea.

Chapter 23

THEY REMINISCED FOR a good while, trading happy memories with each other. Somehow it lessened the pain.

Connor was on his second cup of coffee and more relaxed. He felt content to just sit there, at ease and leaning back on the sofa—listening to the crackling in the fireplace, soaking in the warmth in the cozy room, while looking at the pretty, freshly painted walls.

"Is something else bothering you? You looked worried when you walked in," said Alana.

"And you're perceptive," Connor quipped.

"Care to talk about it? I'm a good listener."

"Well …" Connor glanced at Tom curled in front of the fireplace. He was the scrawny, stray cat his mother loved so dearly, giving him food, nourishing his body until it became strong and healthy. The ferocious cat had preyed on mice, pouncing on the unsuspecting critters, laying them as presents on their doorstep. Tom wasn't content to stay indoors. He was not a bored, fat cat, but a sleek, lean one.

In the last years of his mother's life, it was Tom that

provided companionship for his mother, and it was his adventures and antics that amused her. At night, she took comfort in his presence, always curled next to her in bed. Tom was so much more to her than just a cat. He was family, a companion to his mother. It had been just the two of them. Connor had wrestled with his guilt for not being there, for putting his work ahead of everything else. He would always regret that. His private pain, one he'd live with for the rest of his life. Would he live his life alone—with just Tom?

"Earth to Connor." Alana interrupted his thoughts.

"I messed up," said Connor.

Alana frowned.

"Mary Ann … she did Mother's funeral arrangements. She has a florist shop. That's where I met her." Connor wrung his hands. "I fell in love with her, but I didn't tell her. I went back to the city with Tom and resumed my life there—my job, my condo. I fell into a funk, grieving and in pain. I didn't contact Mary Ann for four months until I came back to see her on Christmas Eve."

"How did she react when she saw you?"

"She was still angry, and hurt. I don't blame her."

"Did you apologize?"

"I tried to, but words seemed futile at that point. It was my actions that hurt her." Connor paused. "I made a mistake, and I regretted it."

"But you never got to tell her how you felt?"

"No," said Connor, his voice cracking. "I was at Mary Ann's house yesterday when my car wouldn't start. I stayed there until this morning. I … I was working up the nerve to tell her, but I didn't get a chance. The tow truck showed up just as I was about to tell her."

Alana sighed. "So that's why the sad look, my friend."

"I haven't gotten to that part yet," said Connor. "On the way back here, I sat in the front of the tow truck and rode back with the driver. Clay couldn't come, so he had someone else help. It was Ron. I know him. We grew up together, and we went to the same school."

"Do you mean Ron, the guy from the hardware store?"

Connor nodded. "He and I … well, we had a talk." Connor fidgeted, then stared into her eyes. "He went out with Mary Ann. They dated."

Alana's eyes were wide now. "I'm sorry, Connor," she said, patting his arm.

"Have I lost her?" An anguished cry escaped from Connor's lips.

Silence filled the room, broken by a few crackles from the burning logs.

Chapter 24

THE NEXT MORNING, Connor squinted his eyes to zoom in on Tom: his body tensed, focused on a bird, out of his reach as he crouched on the sill, peering out the living room window. Almost a month after the visit to Doc Carlson, the spry tomcat's energy had returned, and he sported his old fearless attitude. Coming back home to the small town where he'd lived, to his familiar home, away from the city, Tom had regained weight, and he had gotten his groove back. The vet was right. The only medicine the grieving tabby cat needed was a big dose of love and attention.

Connor had stocked up on cat food, filling two shelves of the pantry with bags of dry food, cans of wet food, and some tasty treats. Digging through the selection of natural cat foods, he located Tom's favorite—salmon and shrimp. He carried it into the kitchen and set it on the counter. Hearing a loud meow, he reached down to scratch behind Tom's ears as the orange tabby greeted him, rubbing his body between Connor's legs.

"Miss me, old man?" said Connor, as he washed Tom's

bowl and dried it with a paper towel.

He popped the lid on the canned cat food. The popping sound and the sudden release of the pungent smell brought out another "Meow," this time louder and throatier.

"Okay, your food is coming," said Connor. He chuckled and grabbed a spoon to scoop it into Tom's bowl.

He watched as Tom licked and nibbled, imagining how he must have looked the first time the cat appeared at the front door, a scraggly stray.

He grinned to nobody in particular. Connor couldn't help it, thinking about her. He recalled the fresh-faced Mary Ann at the breakfast table. Making slow scrambled eggs for her.

His lips parted. Not a timid tilt of his lips, but a broad one that spread across his face, crinkling the corners of his eyes. A smile of pure joy. He held on to the slimmest of hope. Dare he hope again?

Connor replayed the images and clips of Mary Ann and their times together.

He remembered the bead store where she twirled in delight, wearing the new necklace, the hues of her dress and eyes, the colorful gems glittering in the light.

He remembered the flickering candlelight framing her face at Manini's as they lingered and talked over coffee, long after their meal.

He remembered the blush on her cheeks when she ran into him, their shopping carts clashing as they bumped into each other in the grocery store.

He remembered her take-charge attitude as she designed

floral bouquets for his mother's funeral, when he was overwhelmed with grief and was barely able to say the words to describe what he wanted; but she knew, and her fingers communicated his wishes through the beautiful flowers.

He remembered the alarm on her face when their cats went missing as the last guests left Connor's house where he'd hosted a dinner after his mom's funeral. How they frantically searched for Isabella and his Tom.

He added the newer memories, burnt fresh in his mind. Running into Mary Ann at the market, where she picked her soup then forgot it. Bringing it to her home. Sharing a bowl of vegetarian chili while the storm raged outside. Teaching her to play Go Fish, Mary Ann's childlike curiosity, and her delight when she won. Making slow scrambled eggs for her, the best she'd ever had.

Is this what it's like to be in love? Connor wondered. Experiencing the sweet beginnings, the quiet longings, the wisps of hope and yearning. Unspoken, yet always there. Protected and tender. He had never been in love like this before. It'd always been his job that came first—the drive, the energy; it had taken over his life. Until now. At thirty-eight years old, soon to be thirty-nine.

As announcements of marriages and births came and went over the years, Connor never felt rushed. Sure, he had been on dates here and there, and in a couple of semi-serious relationships. He wasn't a eunuch. However, Connor had never experienced feelings like these before. This was different. Special. It wasn't pure lust, the rush of desire that's fleeting or impulsive, over before he knew it with no strings attached, no promises offered or expected.

He'd never brought a girl home to his parents' house. Connor swallowed, keeping the bitterness down. His mother had died, and before that his stepfather. The house was empty. Now, there was no one *to* bring home, and no one here except for him and Tom.

A knock on the door interrupted his thoughts.

Alana stood at the stoop. With her short-cropped hair and natural, no-makeup face, she looked younger than her twenty-five years.

"You've been baking," said Connor, noticing a smudge of flour on her cheek.

"You got that right." She laughed as she walked in, carrying a baking pan wrapped in foil. "Mom and I made pound cake today. You know how she loves to bake. She's been experimenting with the classic pound cake."

"I can't wait to try it." Connor grabbed two plates from the cupboard and cut big slices.

"You have fresh coffee?"

At his nod, Alana grabbed two mugs and poured. She carried them to the dining room table where Connor sat, waiting.

"You're the guinea pig." Alana watched impatiently, waiting for him to take the first bite.

Connor took his sweet time, making a big deal of the test.

Fidgeting in her seat, Alana could hardly contain herself. "Well, what's your verdict?"

"I'm afraid this isn't up to snuff." said Connor solemnly. He dabbed his lips with a napkin.

Alana's jaw dropped.

"Just kidding," said Connor, enjoying her look of amazement. He quickly took another, larger bite and stuffed his mouth full. He savored the taste of the delicious moist cake, rich and creamy, full of flavor. Not dry, heavy and bland. Smacking his lips, he pronounced, "Now that's first-place-ribbon worthy."

"Whew, you had me worried."

"Yum. What's in it?"

"It's amazing what cream cheese and a dollop of sour cream will do."

"I'll be Dottie's guinea pig anytime." Connor washed it down with a gulp of coffee, before leaning back in his chair.

The Alana he saw before him now was more relaxed: her thin, angular face softened. Dottie made up for lost time in the reconciliation with her long-estranged daughter when Alana came home for Christmas. No longer the rebellious waif of seventeen, Alana had grown into a self-assured woman.

Connor had seen the toll exacted on Dottie in the last eight years, magnified by the death of her husband and the abrupt departure of her only child soon after that. Dottie had turned to her neighbor, Connor's mom. They had grown closer; both having lost their husbands. But later, with the passing of his mom, Dottie had faced her grief alone. Last Christmas, Alana had come back, and mother and daughter reunited over tears of forgiveness and joy.

A sense of guilt had swept over Connor. Although he'd come home for the holidays, his visits had become less frequent as time went by. With each passing year, he rationalized his guilt away, convincing himself his mom would be proud of his achievements. It was of little solace to him now, and the decision he made to quit his job and sell his condo was too late. His life in the city had already become a distant memory. Connor had thought he was irreplaceable at work, that they valued his contributions. How wrong he had been. No doubt he had been replaced by another ambitious young man, much like the one he was years ago.

What did he have to show for his life now? In a few months, he'd be thirty-nine. So close to forty. It was depressing to think he'd passed the halfway mark of his life, or perhaps more than that. Had the best years of his life gone, having slaved them away within the steel confines of a cold corporate building? The death of his mother had been a wake-up call. There *had* to be more to life. Connor was not a quitter, and he'd fight for his life, for what was left of it.

"Earth to Connor, hello—"

Alana waved, snapping her fingers to catch his attention.

Chapter 25

CONNOR FELT HER warm breath on his cheek as she leaned in to check on him. He blinked, adjusting his gaze on her face, momentarily fixed on her thick curvy eyelashes.

"You okay?" said Alana.

"I'm fine," he said, shaking his head.

"You lost? Looked like you'd gone somewhere else."

He cleared his throat, glancing around the room. His fingers glided over the smooth laminate of his mother's favorite table. Alana was right. He *was* lost. He'd lost count of the times he sat at the dining room table. Lost sight of his life, his family, what it really meant. Lost the girl. Would he get a second chance?

He'd been a fighter. Quitting hadn't been in his vocabulary, and it would not be. "No." Connor said. He looked her squarely in the eye with a new surge of vitality and determination. "I'm getting my life back, new year and all."

Alana smiled and threw up her arms. "Well, I've been up to my arms in paint! You know, once I finished the living room, Mom wanted me to do the bedrooms."

"You started a big project you'll have to finish." Connor picked up on her enthusiasm, and he saw the flash in her eyes and realized she was enjoying this task, which was bringing mother and daughter closer together. "I'm glad you found this project to your liking." His thoughts turned to Ron, who had bought the hardware store from Connor's dad, and later offered Connor a joint partnership to expand the store. "You've met Ron?"

"Oh yes," nodded Alana. "He's helpful and courteous. We met when I went to pick up paint and supplies. When I told him about my project, he made sure I had everything I needed. Plus, he threw in some tips and said if I ever got in a pickle, to call him."

"I went to school with him. Ron used to work for my dad when he owned the hardware store."

"He's come a long way since. I don't remember him 'cause he's much older than me, and our paths didn't really cross. Not that I'd recognize him though, since I've been gone for eight years," said Alana.

She brushed away the faraway wistful look on her face, and stood up. "Fight for her," said Alana.

Connor stared at Alana, this toughness coming from such a young girl. Leaving home at seventeen, almost homeless on the street, doing what she had to do to survive the eight years on her own.

"You fought for that office with the window."

"This … isn't the same."

"So, you're just going to give up on Mary Ann?"

"No, I don't mean that."

"Look at me, Connor. Tell me you're not a quitter."

"It's not that. If I didn't get that office with the window, I'd try again. I could go out the next day and find work in another company." He paused. "Do you know how many corporate offices are in the city?"

"So that's your excuse?"

"Alana, I *want* a second chance with Mary Ann now. More than anything. I don't want to blow it."

"You won't know until you try."

"Every time I get this close, and I mean *this close*—" Connor leaned in, pinching his thumb and index finger closer, leaving a sliver of a gap. "And I'm almost there, but something gets in the way. Like the other day during the storm … we had breakfast, and I'm getting ready to tell her. So you know what happened?"

"You got tongue-tied?"

"Nope, the tow truck shows up. And it's Ron."

"So, the great Connor is afraid of competition, huh?"

"Bad timing."

Alana shook her head. "I once knew this guy, and he wasn't a macho, super-hunk. Quite the opposite. You wouldn't think of him as the guy who gets the girl. But he had us all fooled."

Connor raised his eyebrow. "How so?"

"We knew he was married. He wore a gold band around his finger. But we didn't know how he got the girl."

"Go on—"

"Well, come to find out, she was already engaged to

another man when they met. But she ended up marrying *this* guy. You've got to hand it to him," said Alana, tilting her head to the side.

"You made your point."

"We were scratching our heads. Go figure."

"Are they happy together?"

"Heck, yes."

"Thanks, my friend." Connor said.

"Win her back," Alana said, as she turned to go.

"You're leaving so soon?"

"I'm going to finish baking with Mother, then do some prep work before tackling the paint job tomorrow," said Alana. She slid the rest of the pound cake onto a plate and gathered her baking pan. "I'll leave the cake with you."

It was a good day, and Connor wouldn't say no to a sweet dessert.

Chapter 26

IT WAS MONDAY morning when Mary Ann reopened her flower shop. She was glad the storm was milder than predicted. The townspeople had prepared for it just in case. They were used to it. The last days of winter, before the spring equinox, were sometimes the worst, as if old man winter huffed and puffed to leave his mark before retreating.

The flower shop was her baby. She loved the smell of fresh flowers, and this was her dream come true. Norma would be here any minute. Mary Ann couldn't sleep, so she got there early. She'd have time to make a quick round and check on everything. She had saved money to buy the walk-in cooler for the flowers she kept in stock. Mary Ann had gotten used to the familiar sound of the refrigeration motors in the back, next to where she created the floral arrangements. Her mind was lost in thought, busy with plans for Valentine's Day and the order for a large shipment of flowers.

Absentmindedly, Mary Ann reached out to open the cooler door, not registering the fact that the blast of air that met her wasn't cold at all. It took a moment before she realized something was wrong. It was quiet. Too quiet. The humming motors were silent.

The power had gone out. The cooler shut down. She took a step toward the first bunch of flowers and her heart sank. The flowers had gotten too hot and wilted. Bending down, her fingers touched the drooping petals. Her knees shook as she took a swift assessment, glancing across the space. "Oh no, how can this be?"

Mary Ann stumbled to the cooler entrance, barely hearing the click as she closed the door. She had put all the flowers in the floral cooler for safekeeping. The storm must have knocked out the electricity. She flicked on the light switches. The lights were out too.

The bell on the door chimed as Norma stepped in. She took one look at Mary Ann's face and knew something was wrong. "You're as pale as a ghost."

"We lost power. The flowers in the cooler are all wilted." Mary Ann's shoulders slumped, her voice trailing.

"Oh no," said Norma, rushing over to Mary Ann to comfort her. "What are we going to do?"

"I don't have orders for today yet. Let's hope the phone won't ring anytime soon before someone calls in an order." Mary Ann looked up, her face animated as an idea popped up. "It's still early. I could go pick up flowers in the city. It'll take me all day, but if I leave now, I may be back late tonight."

"You can make it in one day. But it'll take you longer, with the snow on the road."

"Okay, then please stay here. Call the power company," said Mary Ann, the words rushing out now. "Oh, and can you get a repair guy to come and check the cooler when the electricity is back on? I want to be sure the motor is working fine." Mary Ann switched to action mode, making decisions, finding solutions to take care of the problem.

Norma nodded. "What if the power isn't back on and the cooler isn't working by the time you get back with the flowers?"

"That's a good point," said Mary Ann. She paused, mulling over this with her arms crossed.

"I'll keep you posted while you're on the road."

Mary Ann grabbed her purse and gathered the scarf around her neck as she rushed out the door. "Plan B."

Chapter 27

WALKING CAREFULLY ON the sidewalk, stepping around slippery areas, occasionally crunching snow on the edges of the pavement, Mary Ann made her way to the market a few doors down farther on the street. She breathed a sigh of relief when she saw the lights were on. *Good!* This store had large walk-in coolers in the kitchen and a tall, glass dairy cooler in the front. She quickly sketched out a Plan B as she made her way inside, looking for the manager's office.

"Mary Ann," a voice shouted.

She looked around and saw Connor, waving his arms. Jerking her head up, she slowed down, while her heartbeat speeded up.

"You look like you're in a hurry. Can I help you?"

"I'm looking for the manager."

"Oh, you mean Mrs. Steele," Connor said. "She's the owner and manager. You've met her."

Mary Ann squinted, tilting her head.

"The old lady in your flower shop on Christmas Eve— the one that said to us 'You kids should catch up. No time's better than now.'"

She nodded, putting the name to the face. "I know her."

Connor was grinning, looking over Mary Ann's shoulder. "Here she comes now."

Mary Ann turned around to face her. "Connor was just telling me about you."

"*Good* things?" Mrs. Steele turned to wink at Connor.

Mary Ann chuckled.

"What brings you here?" asked Mrs. Steele as she hugged her in a warm greeting.

Mary Ann touched Mrs. Steele's hand and pointed down the street. "The power is out in my flower shop." She paused, frowning. "This morning when I checked on the flowers in the cooler, they were all wilted."

"My dear, what can I do to help?" Mrs. Steele asked, leaning closer.

"We're contacting the electric company, but there's no telling how long it'll take before the power is back on. We'll need a cooler."

"For your wilted flowers?"

"No, I must order fresh flowers and pick them up in person. That's the quickest way."

"Where?"

"In the city."

"When will you be back?"

"I need to leave now and drive to the city to get back tonight. But with this weather, it'll take longer, and I'll have to drive slower."

"So, you'll need the cooler if you return this evening?"

"Yes, if the power doesn't come back on."

"How much room do you need? I can let you have the dairy cooler in front. I'm afraid we can't put flowers in the kitchen walk-in coolers."

"Thank you, Mrs. Steele. This is a backup plan, just in case. The sooner I leave for the city, the sooner I can come back. I'm not thrilled about driving at night in the dark, especially when I'm not familiar with the road," said Mary Ann.

"I'll go with you. I know the way like the back of my hand," Connor suddenly offered.

Mary Ann's cheeks flushed red. When she found her voice, it was soft. "It's sweet of you to offer, but I can't ask you to do that."

Connor's eyes sparkled. "I've driven that way many times, going back and forth. You helped me with my car; let me at least do this one thing."

Mary Ann felt Mrs. Steele nudge her.

"You kids should *really* catch up. No time's better than now." Mrs. Steele gave them a wink—*again.*

Chapter 28

MARY ANN WASTED no time walking to her car, Connor by her side. She was eager to get started, now that he was going. She hoped Connor didn't see her blush. Had she blushed because of him? Was the quick walk making her breathless, or was it because of Connor?

He seemed different somehow, quieter, after Ron showed up at her house yesterday. She didn't have time to talk to Connor as he'd dashed to get his car ready, scraping the snow off, and helping Ron get it hitched to the tow truck.

Seeing Ron again was unexpected. They remained friends after New Year's Eve, although it was awkward at first. She talked to him about what had happened between them and drew the line to stay in the friend-zone. She tried to be gentle and kind, but firm. He wasn't happy to hear that and called her a few times to convince her otherwise. He stopped by to see her again, but she kept her voice polite and proper, repeating it until he got the message, for good.

"Here we are," said Mary Ann, as they walked up to her car.

Connor reached out for the keys. "I'll drive."

As she handed over her keys, he opened the passenger door for her.

He slid in the driver's side and pushed back the seat, adjusting it to allow for his long legs. The car was roomier on the inside than it appeared at first glance. "You want anything before we get started?"

"Oh, I'm good," said Mary Ann, buckling up. "I want to get on the road."

"We can get something to drink when I stop for gas," said Connor, looking at the needle to see how much gas they had.

Connor had made this trip many times. He knew the roads and was used to driving in the snow.

"I'm glad you came," said Mary Ann.

He smiled, flicking a quick look at her. Connor's heart flipped, beating faster. He concentrated on driving, quickly leaving the small town behind. The highway had been plowed, white mounds piled on the sides turned to dirty gray. He watched for slippery patches, slick areas where the snow was packed down.

"We should make good time with this early start. I'll check the weather before we head back."

They rode in silence for a while, Mary Ann staring at the snowy scenery. It was still cold, but the sunlight shined on the snow, bringing glitter and sparkle. Eyeing the wintery landscape, the beauty of nature took her attention. She could feel her stress and tension drop as the mountain scenery streamed by. Her hands stopped twitching. Her muscles relaxed. Eventually she closed her eyes and rested her head on the seat.

Mary Ann turned her body sideways, tucking her legs in. Her eyelids drooped heavier, strands of hair slipped from her ponytail, a dreamy look drifting on her face. She looked so childlike, fragile, and vulnerable. The Mary Ann the world saw was an independent, smart, self-sufficient businesswoman. She didn't wear her heart on her sleeve. She kept her feelings close to her. Yet underneath throbbed the beating heart of a mature woman capable of and filled with love—love ready to gush out, love that couldn't be measured or contained—for a deserving man, for the right man.

Chapter 29

GAS STATIONS WERE few and far between. Connor had calculated the amount of fuel in the tank and how far it was to the gas station. He passed on the first that came into view. It looked derelict—mounds of snow piled up, trash cans overflowing, litter spilling on the ground, and yellow tape wrapped around a pump.

A road sign indicated the next gas station would be in forty-five miles. A glance at the tank monitor, a third full, assured Connor they would make it there in good shape.

Connor's thoughts turned to Mary Ann. The other day would have been his chance to tell her—or so he'd thought, until Ron turned up. He mulled over his options. Was she Ron's girl now? Had he lost her?

It had been an emotional time for Connor. His grieving heart filled with pain, regret, and guilt. He hadn't been able to forgive himself for a past that he could not change.

This Christmas, unexpectedly, Connor witnessed love, hope, and the power of forgiveness as Mrs. Rainer and Alana reconciled, their lives changing forever. It hadn't come easy;

nothing worthwhile was easy. Dottie and Alana had crossed the dark gulf of pain and heartbreak—swallowed their pride and overcome the anger that pushed them apart—and allowed forgiveness to bring them together, opening their hearts to love again.

This magical Christmas, Connor changed, too. What he witnessed stirred something deep inside him, reaching to the depth of his heart and touching his soul. He moved away from the darkness he had dwelled in, and the thoughtless pain he caused others. He finally forgave himself. He chose a new path, a bright path, one of love—for himself—and the love he would give to others.

Chapter 30

CONNOR DROVE UP to the next gas station. It was bustling with customers, vehicles lined up at the pumps, and more cars parked in front of a small café beside it.

Mary Ann stirred, then arched her back and stretched before sitting up to look out the window.

"Enjoy your nap?"

"Oh, *yeah*." She threw Connor a sheepish grin. "Thanks for letting me sleep so long."

"I'm stopping for gas," said Connor. He gestured to the café sporting a crooked sign tacked on the porch railing, "Wild Horses Roadside Café." "If you want to get us a table, I'll meet you in there."

"Okay, I need to make some calls. Check with Norma," said Mary Ann.

It took a few minutes for Connor to fill up the gas and pay. He hopped back in the car and parked in front of the café.

Walking up the steps, Connor opened the door to the smell of strong coffee, sizzling food on the grill, and the distinct odor of frying onions. The clinking of utensils on plates, the hollering of orders, and the chatter of talk melted into the amorphous noise of a busy café. Somebody coughed. Laughter drifted. He scanned the room, looking for Mary Ann. She was sitting at a table by the far wall and waved him over, keeping an eye on him as she talked on her cell phone.

Connor pulled out a chair, noticing the cheap padding had split, the stuffing exposed. As he sat down, she finished her call. "Good news?"

"The power company is working on it. They will try to get it fixed as soon as possible."

"Can you salvage the flowers?"

"I'm afraid not. Norma is throwing them out. But I have some good news. I just called the flower shop in the city to place an order. It'll be on the delivery truck headed our way. We can meet them here."

"When?"

"About three hours. It'll save us from driving the six-hour round trip there and back. They deliver to shops in this area anyway. When I explained the situation, the lady on the phone was so nice. She said it'll be no trouble at all to make an extra stop at the café."

"I'm glad that worked out."

"Perfectly."

"Have you ordered?"

"Just coffee for us, the waitress will be back to take our food order."

Connor relaxed, leaning back in his chair, toying with his

napkin. What a stroke of luck to be here with Mary Ann. Different from Manini's, this greasy spoon had its own charm. Scratched wood tabletops, worn-out chairs, scuffed flooring trodden by countless feet—the café had welcomed many travelers over the years. On the wall hung a framed black-and-white photo of The Rolling Stones. He felt at ease, being here. Was this the right place ... and time? Would Connor have the courage—here and now—to tell Mary Ann that he loved her?

The waitress brought two mugs of coffee, sloshing and spilling some as she set them on the table in her haste, clutching a pad.

"Ready to order?"

Connor nodded at Mary Ann, waiting for her to go first.

"How's your grilled cheese sandwich?"

"Ma'am, it's good. The cook piles on lots of cheese so it's thick and gooey."

"I'll take it. And a small cup of your vegetable soup, please," said Mary Ann, as she handed back the sticky menu with brown stains and bent corners.

"And you sir, what'll you have?"

"I'll have the biscuits and gravy with hash browns and fried eggs."

The waitress nodded and picked up his menu. "Coming right up."

Chapter 31

THE FOOD WAS every bit as good as he hoped. Connor ate quickly, finishing before Mary Ann did. "How was your grilled cheese sandwich?"

"It was perfect—crisp and crunchy on the outside, soft and gooey on the inside." Mary Ann grinned as she wiped her greasy fingers on the paper napkin before cutting into the thick slices of red tomatoes on her plate, the juice and seeds spilling out.

He watched as Mary Ann dipped her spoon into the soup, scooping up the liquid, tipping the bowl slightly to get the last drops at the bottom. He was a fast eater and finished first; he liked to watch her, observing her good table manners.

She dabbed the napkin on her lips and pushed back the bowl.

"Don't tell me you like this better than mine," said Connor, making a face, pretending to look hurt.

"If I did, I wouldn't tell you," Mary Ann retorted, giving a wink as she said, "But you got serious competition."

Connor sat up in his chair. "I'm a big boy, I can take it." He enjoyed seeing her light, playful side. Giggles had replaced the frowns from earlier this morning.

The ringing of his cell phone interrupted Connor's thoughts. He answered it.

"Hey, Clay here. Looked at your SUV."

"What's wrong?"

"It's your battery. I can order you a new one, but it may take two or three days to get here."

Connor sighed with relief as he ended the call. "Okay, thanks, man."

The waitress came by to refill their coffees. "Anything else I can get you?" She paused. "We have homemade brownies, thick double chocolate. Topped with vanilla ice cream."

Connor was not one to pass up dessert, especially *double* chocolate brownies—his favorite chocolaty dessert. "Sure, I'll have one. Mary Ann?"

She nodded. "Make it two."

The waitress reappeared as they finished their dessert, clearing their plates, and bringing more coffee.

"Thank you. It was delicious," said Connor.

Mary Ann echoed her "thanks" as the waitress refilled their coffee mugs and left.

Connor cleared his throat. "Mrs. Steele said we should catch up. You know … have a little chat." He looked up at her. Connor thought he saw a twinkle in Mary Ann's eyes. He relaxed, breathing easier now, and leaned back in his chair. So far so good.

"Well, I also heard her say 'No time's better than now,' and she's darn right," said Mary Ann. "So, you're back. What are your plans?"

"Take it easy for now. I've got enough money to do that for a while."

"How do you feel about coming back?"

"Honestly? I feel great. I have more freedom to sleep in, to make my schedule or not have one at all. I'll never put my nose to the grindstone again for anyone other than myself."

"Be your own boss."

"Exactly. I have to take care of myself. Eat healthy food, exercise, and reduce stress. All the stuff I know I need to do. You know I'm almost thirty-nine and older than you."

"By six years … yeah." Mary Ann giggled.

"Your time will come, young lady," Connor teased.

"Do you have hopes and dreams?"

"I've been thinking about my mother. You remember that wooden recipe box of hers?"

Mary Ann nodded, recalling the time they cooked together in his kitchen.

"I've been experimenting with new recipes, cooking with different foods, textures, and flavors—inspired by her recipes. I'd like to put together a cookbook and dedicate it to her."

"What a wonderful tribute to your mother," said Mary Ann, clapping softly.

Connor gulped his coffee. His mother and father were both gone, but the throbbing pain remained, still a fresh wound. There were days when it hurt so much he almost couldn't bear it. "I remember one time, when my mother had an injury and couldn't walk, my father carried her. In the morning when she woke up, he'd help her go to the bathroom, get dressed, and carry her to the living room. He did everything for her, including bathing her."

"Did he complain?"

"Not to her. But the effort and the exertion took its toll on him from the way he walked, the dark shadows under his eyes, and how tired he looked." Connor's lips quivered. "Mom referred to him as her 'big teddy,' usually when she didn't think I was around. He was a tall, big guy, and she loved it when he gave her a bear hug." He smiled, recalling the fond memory. "They acted quite proper around me, no kissing, nothing like that. But they gave each other hugs. There was no shortage of hugs."

"So sweet."

"Even after all those years." Connor nodded. "He loved her. Adored her so much he'd do anything for her."

"Anything?"

"Yes, he raised me—like a father." Connor paused, his glance steady as his voice quivered. "Even though I wasn't *his.*"

Chapter 32

"I RODE WITH Ron in the tow truck. He told me you've been dating. But I want to hear it from you." Connor spoke quietly.

"After you left, I went out with Ron. We had a few dates … and we spent the Christmas holidays together."

"Are you still seeing him?"

"I … well, *no*."

"You ended it?" Connor's heart skipped a beat, as he reminded himself not to celebrate prematurely.

"On our last date … we kissed—"

He had clenched his teeth so hard, grinding the molars. Jealousy sprang and caught him in its claws. Connor had a sudden urge to lash out. A kiss? He didn't want to go there. He closed his eyes, but he could still see them in his mind. Was it a shy, furtive kiss? Was it demanding and seeking? Did she kiss him back? Did she enjoy it?

He'd dreamt of the moment their lips touched. It would begin with a sweet, slow kiss that weakened his knees and sent a surge of warmth spreading through his body. A tender kiss. A firm kiss.

"—but I knew then it wasn't what I wanted," said Mary Ann, finishing her sentence.

He wanted to step in and take her, swoop her into his arms. In his mind she had been his, always his. Connor knew what *he* wanted, but his attempts to tell Mary Ann had failed each time, slipping through his fingertips.

Chapter 33

THE CROWD HAD thinned at the café, but to the couple with heads bent forward, eyes focused on each other, lost in conversation—it seemed like it was just the two of them. Nearby, music played softly from the coin-operated jukebox.

"What *do* you want, Mary Ann?"

"You know those old couples walking and holding hands?" She smiled with her lips and her eyes, meeting his in a shy gaze.

"Like they're still sweethearts," said Connor.

"I see their wizened hands and gnarled fingers, their thin, lined faces, and their weary feet, dragging and moving slowly, with an effort," said Mary Ann, almost in a whisper. "But they touch each other, not letting go. It's as if they exist together. Isn't that real love?"

"Some people aren't so demonstrative," said Connor with a shrug, thinking of his own parents. "There are other ways. Small acts of love showing how they care for each other. Thoughtful things. It doesn't have to be dramatic, or showy, or expensive."

"I want the love that lasts forever. I believe it exists, long after our physical bodies turn to dust. A love so strong it joins our souls together."

"I apologize for hurting you," said Connor. He held up his hand. "Please hear me out. I've been selfish. I was in a dark place since my mother died, and I didn't want to bring you into my world. But I also hurt you. I realize it now—that in keeping the distance and pushing you away, I increased your pain. I'm so sorry."

Mary Ann was quiet.

"In the end, when I look back on my life, I don't want to have regrets," said Connor. His chin quivered as he spoke. "I can't go back and change the past and agonizing over it won't help."

Mary Ann saw the intensity in his eyes. She heard the sincerity in his voice and the rawness of his emotions.

"Can you find it in your heart to forgive me?"

The bitterness that Mary Ann had carried tore her up like a sharp thorn, pricking and drawing blood as long as she held the grudge. Connor had asked for her forgiveness before, but she had hardened her heart—holding herself above him, as if she was the righteous one and he, the sinner. But it gave her no pleasure. She dropped her head in shame.

"I'm sorry," whispered Connor. He would ask her for forgiveness a thousand times rather than hurt her again.

A tear trickled down her cheeks. Connor's heart sank at the thought that he'd caused her to cry. He felt helpless, afraid he'd made it worse. He lifted her chin and wiped away the drops gently with his thumb.

Mary Ann struggled to find her voice. "Can you forgive *me?*"

Connor reached across the table and sought Mary Ann's hand, his fingertips curling around hers.

Mary Ann didn't pull away—through the warmth of his hands flowed the strength of Connor's love. She saw the confirmation in his eyes.

Connor swallowed. "I want you beside me—*always.*"

She turned her hand around reaching for his, her palm facing Connor's, bending her fingers to clasp around his fingers.

"I love you," Connor croaked, his voice raw and raspy, as he scooted his chair next to Mary Ann and put his arm around her shoulder, drawing her closer. They stayed that way, without speaking, for a long while. Tenderness and love welled up inside him and filled his heart. He had let her in his heart—and he'd never let her go.

Chapter 34

A SONG PLAYED on the jukebox—soulful and heart-wrenching, yet infused with sweetness and hope.

Mary Ann's eyes misted over, as she turned to Connor and whispered softly, "I love you."

"I love you, too." He reached for her fingers and kissed the back of her hand.

She smiled and glanced at the couple dancing near the jukebox: their bodies melded together, moving as one to the music.

"Dance with me," Connor breathed in her ear, as his lips brushed against Mary Ann's hair, inhaling her fresh citrus scent. He stood up, holding her hand, not letting go, and led her to a cleared area in front of the jukebox.

Mary Ann felt the touch of Connor's hands, and then his body, as she leaned in—yielding to him, letting him take the lead.

Their movements became smoother as their feet, awkward at first, stepped in sync to the music.

Mary Ann closed her eyes, secure in Connor's arms,

swaying to the hauntingly beautiful melody. Happiness engulfed her, swelling from deep inside, transporting her home to a place she had longed to go, where her heart throbbed, beating strong and steady.

She rested her head on his shoulder.

He tucked a wisp of loose hair behind Mary Ann's ears.

Connor held her in a tender grip, spilling his love into her and feeling the love returned as she hugged back, embracing him. It was just the two of them now—arms wrapped around each other—slow dancing.

When the song ended, he didn't let go. They stayed in the small cleared area in front of the brightly lit jukebox.

Connor raised his head, hearing coins dropping in the coin slot on the jukebox. Displayed on the screen was "Compact Disc" in big letters on the first line, and underneath it, three lines in smaller lettering: "3 plays for $1.00, 7 plays for $2.00, 18 plays for $5.00."

The waitress made a selection, pushing the first button, "Press for Most Popular Selection." She walked by them as "Wild Horses" played again, smiling as she said in passing, "We like to keep the music going."

Epilogue
THREE MONTHS LATER

Chapter 35

IT WAS A beautiful April morning. Connor watched Tom frolic outside as he felt the warmth of the sun and smelled the freshness sprinkled by a spring shower, awakening the earth from the long cold months of hibernation. He inhaled deeply, taking in the fresh, after-rain smell.

He almost envied Tom and his carefree life. Yesterday he had taken the tabby cat to see Doc Carlson. This time, Connor knew that he didn't need to worry. Over the last few months, Tom had gradually returned to his old self—chasing butterflies, watching birds, catching mice, nibbling on blades of grass, stopping to investigate a new nook or cranny, and napping outside.

It hadn't been easy, and the two of them had struggled together. It was a hard journey—especially early on, in the dark days when he felt too depressed to come out of his shell and take care of Tom. Some days, he'd rather stay in bed, and not face the world. Tom's spirit had a lightening effect on Connor, and he returned it with affection and as much love as you can give to a cat—a member of the family.

Friday nights became date night. Connor would pick up Mary Ann, and they'd go out to dinner. More often than not, it was at Manini's.

He paid more attention to his appearance. He showered, meticulously groomed, and splashed on his favorite aftershave. A sharp dresser from years in a corporate environment, Connor had donated his expensive suits, ties, and buffed, shiny leather dress shoes before he left the city. Still sharply dressed, his new wardrobe of stylish, casual clothing accentuated the trim, muscular build underneath.

They'd check out what movies were playing in the town's only theater, which had two small screens. Connor would let Mary Ann pick the movie. He preferred action or thrillers. Although Connor wasn't into the mushy movies, he went along with her—that was what Mary Ann wanted to see. Seated, he'd take her small hand in his, his arm reaching across Mary Ann's seat to find it resting in her lap.

For years, Connor rarely went to the movies when he lived in the city. The theaters there were monstrous caverns with high ceilings and long, sloped aisles. When he had a hankering to see a first-run action blockbuster that was playing, he'd slip in the back of the theater and watch it alone. He felt swallowed up in the darkness among strangers—as if he didn't belong.

Now he couldn't wait for Friday nights. With Mary Ann by his side, Connor no longer felt alone. They belonged there, in a theater full of lovers in the dark—hands clasping, fingers entwined, shoulders touching, and the excited giggles—like they were experiencing the magic of the big screen for the first time.

Bridget Jones's Diary was one of Mary Ann's favorites. And so, when the latest film in the series came out, they went to see the movie the first night it was showing. Connor was there as Mary Ann laughed and cried her way through the romantic comedy. He glimpsed her face, lit by bright flashes of images flickering on the screen, heard her sniffles, and saw the wetness on her cheeks when she teared up. Although Connor wouldn't admit it, he found himself silently cheering for Mark Darcy.

Connor was a man used to taking charge. He had excelled in his job in the city, rising to the corporate management levels. He was still that guy—and letting Mary Ann choose movies was an act of love. Connor could no longer be selfish and insist on having his way. Nor did he want to.

They were standing in line to get the movie tickets, a few weeks later on another Friday night, when Mary Ann made a suggestion as they moved up to the ticket window. She spoke up when they reached the teller. Connor thought he had heard wrong, asking her to repeat it, but her voice was firm. The movie she chose was an action thriller, an international blockbuster with his favorite actor in the leading role.

Chapter 36

PLAYING CARDS WITH Mary Ann also became a favorite pastime, chasing away the gloom of the wintry evenings. After that first time, it became a weekly event. A tradition that started by chance and turned into a fixture in their routine. Every Sunday night. Quick to catch on, Mary Ann proved a worthy adversary. At first, he'd chalked it up to beginner's luck, but that streak kept going. More often than not, she'd beat him.

A few weeks in, one day Mary Ann casually asked him to come earlier so they could cook dinner together before the card games. Connor was pleased at this unexpected invite, and he shopped at the market to pick out the freshest fruits and vegetables. During the week, he experimented with new recipes or practiced making dishes from old ones his mother had kept in the wooden recipe box in the kitchen.

Sunday dinners became special as Connor looked forward to seeing Mary Ann. Eventually he even brought Tom, who quickly became reacquainted with Isabella. At first, there was a bit of hissing and loud meows. Isabella wasn't used to sharing her space. She held her nose in the air and acted like a prissy princess, but Tom would have none of it. He made himself at home.

The day Isabella first met Tom, Mary Ann had been invited to dinner at Connor's home and had carried her cat in her arms. Isabella had caught sight of Tom sprawled on Connor's couch in the living room. Then Tom gave a low growl, short and throaty, as Isabella slipped out of Mary Ann's grasp and leapt on the couch, landing close to his orange-striped tail as he flicked it in the air. She swiped at it, a few hairs brushing the tips of her claws. Isabella sniffed such delectable new smells—a faint masculine scent, dirt, and a bit of the wild. A strong, heady smell of someone who traveled off the beaten path.

Isabella had been an indoor cat most of her life. Used to the confines of her home, she remained content to prowl familiar territory—her paws sinking in the plush carpeting in the bedroom cushioned by countless acrylic fibers underneath; the click of her toenails as she padded her way across the cold smooth tiles of the kitchen and the hardwoods in the living room.

She was never one to get her paws dirty. After all, she was a beautiful white cat, her fur impeccably groomed.

One day, while playing cards, Mary Ann pointed toward the couch. Both of the cats were lounging on it, each taking up their space, yet a part of their bodies touched, almost overlapping like a Venn diagram. The cats were quiet, not fighting. Connor stifled a grunt and winked.

Connor stepped outside, kicking his shoes off. His feet sank into the wet blades of grass. He ran after Tom, feeling the freedom and the odd sensation of bare feet on the lawn. He skipped, turning around as he spread his arms. Connor closed his eyes and lifted his face toward the sun, seeking its warmth and energy.

If he lived in another era, Connor would be riding a horse bareback, hair blowing in the wind. Or he'd be drumming, the rhythmic pounding on the rawhide-stretched drum pulsating with the wild beating of his heart. He felt savagely free, connected with life around him—the flowers, plants, trees, wild critters, even the insects that fly or the bugs that crawl. The drops of spring rain nourished him, lifting his spirits. Raising his eyes toward the sky, he looked up to the heavens, sending a silent message to his mother. A message of love, strength, and raw desire to survive, to live.

Connor had stifled the feelings of hopelessness and despair. Fear too, of being left alone in this world, with no one to call family except for the cat. The long nights of sleeplessness as he tossed and turned in his childhood bed, watching the gentle rise and fall of Tom's chest. He felt tenderness wash over him, listening to the soft breathing of this cat curled and nestled next to him, its pink nose half-buried in the comforter. Connor's heart filled with wonder—this precious, living being, this scruffy orange tabby cat, had managed to show him what love is without uttering a single word.

It had been almost a month of April showers, bringing forth life in the world around them. May was around the corner. The stirring outside awakened Connor's dormant heart. Opening his heart to feel, to love, baring it to emotions he had clamped down. Two sides of a coin. Love and pain. Baring his heart and soul would mean risking it all, opening it to loss, hurt, and pain.

Time hadn't erased the pain and grief he felt after the death of his mother. It had eased, but it had never gone.

He turned and walked slowly back home, pausing in the doorway. Sunlight beamed on the bare wooden floors and brightened the living room. In the distance, he heard the birds singing. Their caws belting loudly, wings flapping fearless and high over the treetops. As if they were calling him, urging him to join them in living.

Chapter 37

THEY HAD DINNER with family and friends last night. Mary Ann had made it clear to her mother that her stepfather wasn't invited. Her mother had made the trip alone. Connor had invited his best friend, Mark, from the city to spend the weekend. They had met at the community college, shortly after Connor moved to the city, and kept in touch after they graduated and found jobs. Mark had brought his younger sister, Deb. Mary Ann took an instant liking to her. They quickly became friends, chatting away as if they'd known each other forever.

Mary Ann glanced at the alarm clock next to her bed, before jumping in the shower and getting dressed. Connor would be here soon to pick her up for the short drive to the cemetery to pay their respects to his parents. She had made two bouquets of spring flowers to place at their graves. Mary Ann quickly applied a dash of eyeshadow, using a new shade of violet she'd just bought. She didn't fiddle with her hair, leaving it down to be styled later.

Chapter 38

THE GARDEN WAS transformed into a magical place of beauty for the late-afternoon event. Sparkling lights were strung among the trees. The patio area was decorated with lights and lanterns, and dotted with tables covered with white tablecloths with a strip of burlap running down the middle. Glass vases of colorful spring wildflowers, hand-picked and fresh, decorated each table, each floral centerpiece a beautiful creation of nature's art that rested next to scented candles.

An area was cleared in the middle for the dance. Speakers had been erected overlooking the patio, with a table for the DJ.

Alongside the patio, a row of tables was lined up for the food and drinks. Manini's catered the food—*Calamari Fritti, Eggplant Parmigiana, Linguini Clams,* and salads. Wild Horses Roadside Café catered the dessert. Homemade brownies, thick double chocolate with vanilla ice cream.

The wedding cake was a special creation inspired by a recipe from Connor's mom: layered with berries inside, a luscious buttercream icing wrapped the round cake, topped with fresh fruit and sprigs of green leaves.

Ice-filled tall glassware held drinks: a Shirley Temple with lemon-lime soda and a splash of grenadine, or a Mojito with fresh lime juice, garnished with mint leaves and lime wedges.

A walkway connected the patio to a grassy area, surrounded by trees and flowers. An arch stood erected at the beginning of the path. Its latticed wood intertwined with beautiful blossoms and green vines. Pink rose petals were scattered along the pathway from the arch to the patio. The scent of flowers fragranced the air.

Connor stood by the arch as he waited with Pastor Maller, facing the seated guests as the flute and violin music played. In the front row sat Mary Ann's mom, Eva Maller, Mrs. Dottie Rainer and Alana. Behind them sat Norma and Stan and their kids, Mrs. Steele, Doc Carlson, and Mark and Deb. Mikey and Sally and their two boys and even Dale Williams, Mr. Monroe and Ron were also present, sitting among other invited guests.

Connor looked sharp in a tux, his slim body fit and lean. A boutonniere was pinned on the lapel. His heart beat faster in anticipation of seeing Mary Ann any minute now, as the music changed to the *Wedding March*.

She looked radiant, wearing a flower crown in her long, flowing hair and dressed in a white lace, floral print dress. Mary Ann walked slowly down the path, carrying a beautiful bridal bouquet.

Mary Ann and Connor were united on a gorgeous day, favored by a warm, bright sun, a clear blue sky, the caress of a gentle spring breeze, and the chirping of songbirds. As the beaming Pastor Maller pronounced them husband and wife, he said, "You may kiss."

Champagne glasses were raised in toast as the wedding party moved to the reception in the garden. As the happy couple, Mr. and Mrs. Connor Norton, mingled among the guests celebrating and laughing, Tom and Isabella frisked and frolicked together in the garden.

Author's note

I hope you've enjoyed *Second Chance* and the *Flowers in December* series.

Thanks for coming along Connor and Mary Ann's journey to find their happily ever after!